RUNNING
on the
ROOF
of the
WORLD

RUNNING

on the

ROOF

of the

WORLD

JESS BUTTERWORTH

ALGONQUIN YOUNG READERS   2018

Published by
Algonquin Young Readers
an imprint of Algonquin Books of Chapel Hill
Post Office Box 2225
Chapel Hill, North Carolina 27515-2225

a division of
Workman Publishing
225 Varick Street
New York, New York 10014

First published in Great Britain in 2017 by Hodder and Stoughton.

Printed in the United States of America.

Published simultaneously in Canada by Thomas Allen & Son Limited.

Design by Carla Weise.

LIBRARY OF CONGRESS CATALOGING-IN-PUBLICATION DATA

Names: Butterworth, Jess, author.
Title: Running on the roof of the world / Jess Butterworth.
Description: First edition. | Chapel Hill, North Carolina :
Algonquin Young Readers, 2018. | First published in Great Britain in 2017
by Hodder and Stoughton. | Summary: After her parents are arrested by
Chinese soldiers because of their religious beliefs, twelve-year-old Tash
and her best friend Sam travel from their home in Tibet across the
Himalayas to India in order to seek the help of the Dalai Lama.
Identifiers: LCCN 2017046890 (print) | LCCN 2017050884 (ebook) |
ISBN 9781616208349 (ebook) |
ISBN 9781616208196 (hardcover : alk. paper)
Subjects: | CYAC: Freedom of religion—Fiction. |
Government, Resistance to—Fiction. | Voyages and travels—Fiction. |
Survival—Fiction. | Adventure and adventurers—Fiction. | Refugees—Fiction. |
Tibet Autonomous Region (China)—Fiction. | China—Fiction. |
LCGFT: Action and adventure fiction.
Classification: LCC PZ7.1.B895 (ebook) | LCC PZ7.1.B895 Ru 2018 (print) |
DDC [Fic]—dc23
LC record available at https://lccn.loc.gov/2017046890

10 9 8 7 6 5 4 3 2 1

First Edition

*To everyone who has ever
felt too small to make a
difference*

Author's Note

I spent much of my childhood living in the foothills of the Himalayas with my parents and grandparents. My grandma would take my hand and tell me stories of her adventures: how she traveled to India by boat at ten years old, gardened with the Dalai Lama when he first arrived, and encountered many animals. There was the black bear that stole the dog food, the leopard cub my uncle rescued and rehabilitated, and the monkey that would climb into bed with everyone.

Soon, one of my favorite things to do was clamber over the mountains searching for wildlife and imagining that I was on my own adventures in the wilderness.

As I got older, I met Tibetans who explained how they had walked for months across the Himalayas, risking their lives to escape from Tibet into India.

These stories inspired *Running on the Roof of the World*.

—Jess Butterworth

RULES

My feet pound against the gravelly path as I dash through the barley fields enclosed by the mountains. The wind bites, stinging my nose and cheeks. When I've been stuck in school all day, racing Sam home is my favorite thing to do.

I stick my arms out and soar like the golden eagles. My fingers rustle the barley stems. It disturbs the stinkbugs and they fly out, buzzing into the air. My schoolbag thuds against my back.

"Tash," Sam shouts. "Stop!"

I'm not falling for that again. I focus on the uneven ground, dodging the stones and leaping across the dips in the earth. Falling over now would be the ultimate defeat.

"Soldiers," hisses Sam. "Please stop, Tash!"

I raise my head and my stomach drops. Thirty yards ahead are three soldiers. I recognize them immediately: Spaniel, Wildface, and Dagger.

I dig my heels into the earth, but my right foot slips and I crash to the ground.

Sam's footsteps slow behind me.

"Are you all right?" he whispers.

I nod and hold my breath, willing the soldiers to keep walking.

Rule Number One: Don't Run in Front of a Soldier.

Spaniel turns, his hand on his rifle. He spots me and taps Dagger on the shoulder.

They stride toward us, getting closer and closer. Three hard faces glower at me. I lower my eyes to the ground, fighting the urge to glance up.

Rule Number Two: Never Look at a Soldier.

The pebbles crunch under their heavy boots.

"Get up," hisses Sam, shaking my shoulder.

I can't get my body to move.

The footsteps slow. The soldiers bend over me.

"What's going on here?" asks Dagger softly.

Sam's hand is gripping my arm. I stand on shaky legs before them.

"Going home," I say. "I tripped."

Rule Number Three: Say as Little as Possible. They always try to catch you out.

"You know it's against the regulations to run?" Spaniel's nose twitches. His rifle points straight at me.

Everyone at school says he can sniff out anybody who has broken the rules.

"Maybe we should take you to the Wujing and you can tell them where you were running to?" he says.

People taken to the Wujing police never return.

Sam's eyes dart about and I know he's hunting for an escape route. We could dash into the fields but with all the checkpoints they'd soon find us.

"What about you?" asks Spaniel, pressing his face close to Sam's. "You think you can run and get away with it?"

Sam's breathing is heavy.

Spaniel stays rooted to the spot for what feels like forever. I look upward. The wind dies down and the clouds pause in the sky, waiting for something to snap.

Garbled voices blare from the satellite phone slung onto Dagger's belt. He raises it to his ear and turns to the others. "The crowd's too big at the market. They need backup."

"We'll be watching you," Spaniel warns. "Come on. Let's go."

The soldiers march back down the path into town. I want to run and scream and kick at them. But I stay silent, clenching my fists.

"Are you okay?" I ask.

Sam nods. "You?"

"Yeah," I say, hearing my voice quaver.

We all have our ways of protesting against the soldiers. Mom sings songs about what it was like when she was a child, before they arrived. Dad scribbles cryptic leaflets for the resistance movement.

As for me? There are two words that are banned in Tibet. Two words that can get you locked in prison without a second thought. I think these words often. Sometimes I even say them.

I watch the soldiers tramping away and call the words after them.

"Dalai Lama."

CROWD

My words melt into the air, up to the snowy Himalayas around us. My skin tingles. The Dalai Lama is the leader of my people. When I say his name it's as if he's protecting me, all the way from India, where he lives in exile.

"I can't believe you just said that," Sam says.

"What?" I ask, snapping a piece of barley in half and picking at the kernels. "You say it too."

"Never with soldiers near! Do you know how close that was?"

I kick at the pebbles, scattering them. Sam doesn't look different but recently he's changed.

I realize we've stopped in the middle of the path.

Rule Number Four: Don't Draw Attention to Yourself.

"Walk next to me," I say.

Sam waits while I catch up to him. We walk in unison, taking slow steps. I hum to myself, like Mom does, trying to be as ordinary as possible.

The winding path home takes forever. Sam's silence makes it drag.

We're almost at the checkpoint before the corner into the main square. There's a fence to ensure that everyone going in and out of town is monitored. I reach in my pocket for my school papers.

Sam halts and raises his arm to stop me.

"There's no one there," he says.

I creep closer.

Sam's right. The chairs are empty. One of them has fallen on its back.

"Where did they go?" I ask.

I scan the land around us, spotting the purple skirts of women bent over in the fields picking out the weeds. A yak herder whistles beside the stream trickling down from the glaciers. There's no sign of any soldiers.

"Should we wait?" asks Sam.

The mining trucks growl in the distance.

"Let's go," I say, crossing in front of the checkpoint. "We need to get home."

Just as we pass, sirens blare close by.

"It must be coming from town!" shouts Sam. He grabs my hand, pulling me past the fence.

We race around the corner and into the main square.

Usually after school the square is busy with people shopping, sharing food, and laughing.

But today it's different. Everyone is gathered in the middle, pressed against each other. They face the same direction, watching something. Silence ripples through the group and there are no smiles.

I stand on the edge, where the crowd is thinner, and scan faces, checking for Mom and Dad. An old lady holding hands with two toddlers hurries past us, away from everyone. I spot Dad's friend Dorjee, who always gives me a lump of rock sugar to share with Sam when I buy supplies for Mom. He's walking stiffly into the huddle of people.

Soldiers wrestle their way through the crowd, gripping their rifles. I swallow, trying to ignore the sinking feeling in the pit of my stomach. We stop next to the vegetable shop. People scramble to get a better view of the commotion. Someone knocks over a box and carrots tumble across the dirt.

"What's happening?" I ask, and stand on tiptoes. A man shakes his head. I still can't see.

I look for Sam. He's gone. Lost in the mass of people.

I push past a group of women, grasping at their striped dresses.

"Let me through!" I cry as I dart in and out of the bodies.

Finding an opening, I burst out of the crowd. A wall of heat rushes against my face. I see a fireball in the street.

In the middle of the flames is a man.

FLAMES

For a split second I don't think it's real.

The man stands, gripping a Tibetan flag over his head. Flames lick the corners of the fabric and they curl as the red ink bleeds into the blue and yellow. He looks to the sky and shouts. My ears are ringing. The edges of my vision blur.

The Man on Fire steps forward and flames cling to his body. He runs past Dorjee's camping shop, leaving a trail of thick smoke. His mouth is wide and roaring.

The crowd draws back and my mind begins working again.

The Man on Fire races down the street, past the shop selling copper teapots. Flames swirl around him.

The crowd fights to get out of the way.

Fire rips through the flag above the man's head. The flag tears down the middle.

The women next to me are watching, hands in front of their mouths.

"Why is no one doing anything?" I whisper.

I can't tear my eyes away. The man stumbles and falls onto his hands and knees. The flag has burnt away.

In seconds, soldiers are all over the Man on Fire, smothering the flames under blankets. They shove the onlookers back, bundle him up, and steal him away in an army truck.

The crowd is alive.

"He did it to himself."

"He doused himself in flames."

I'm wedged between two men and their weight crushes my chest. A hand grips my arm. It's Sam.

"Follow me," he says.

I scramble forward, squinting through stinging eyes. In every breath I taste burning.

I reach the shops and lean on a basket of iron pots to steady myself. Barely stopping, I sprint up the track and fly past the rows of square stone houses with flat roofs cut into the side of the mountain.

Our front door is open and I spot Mom in the kitchen. I dash past the house and climb the mountain, scrabbling at the jagged rock. I heave myself onto the flat ground. The river gushes below. The back of my throat burns.

Who was that man?

Why did he set himself on fire?

In the distance the late sunlight catches the twisted branches of the vulture tree. The twigs dissolve into flames. I blink. It's not real.

Something touches my shoulder and I jump away. The wind blows wisps of hair across Sam's face. They stick to the sweat on his broad cheekbones.

I let my body sink onto the cold stone.

Sam squats down next to me. We sit in silence, listening to the wind roar.

SHADOW

"**W**e need to find your dad," says Sam. "He'll know what to do."

I nod in agreement. When we were younger we thought the same thing so often that we pretended we could read each other's minds.

Dad will help the Man on Fire. He has to.

I hear the thud of footsteps. Kalsang, our neighbor, rushes down the path. His coat is unbuttoned and flaps behind him.

"Have you seen Tinley?" he asks.

"Not since school," I say, brushing my hands together. The dirt sprinkles onto the ground.

Kalsang scans the ridge.

"What about you?" he asks Sam.

Sam shakes his head apologetically.

Kalsang hastens onward, heading down toward the river, dodging the goats wandering across the path.

As we hurry toward the houses, I scratch my hand on the wall of branches stacked at the side to stop the goats from straying. Ahead, chimney smoke rises into the clear sky. Winter will be here soon.

Another neighbor, Dolka, is hunched over a spindle in front of her house, spinning yak's wool. A carved walking stick rests against the axle. Her long gray hair is parted neatly down the middle and swept into a bun. She hears us and looks up.

"Get inside, Tashi-la," she says. "There's a curfew tonight."

The sun is setting behind the monastery on the slope opposite us. The rectangular rooms are etched into the gray mountain like steps. At the top stands the temple.

No one will be allowed outside after dark.

"The sun will be gone in thirty minutes," says Sam.

I spot flashes of dark red as the monks walk in

and out of the rooms. I used to dream of becoming a nun, until Mom told me I'd have to live in the monastery forever and shave my head. After that I changed my mind, but I still stood next to the stone building whenever I could. If I got close enough I would lean against the cool stone, catching whiffs of thick incense and snippets of deep prayers.

I am lost in the memory; it's easier than thinking about anything else right now.

"Tashi-la," says Dolka, "you should listen to your elders." She bends over, reaches into the woven basket, and wraps a new piece of wool around her fingers.

"Sorry," I mumble. "We're going now."

There's movement at the bottom of the monastery. Rows of soldiers march up to the base and gather around the building like a shadow. My heart thumps.

"Not the monastery," says Dolka, letting the wool drop to the ground. "Please, not them."

"Tash!"

I know that voice. It's Mom. She strides toward me, gathers me in her arms, and hugs me so tightly I can hardly breathe.

"I told her to go inside," says Dolka.

"Thank you," says Mom, loosening her grip.

She squeezes Dolka's hand. "You should go inside too."

Mom glances at the monastery. It's surrounded by soldiers. They're camouflaged against the gray rock.

"Quickly," says Mom, gesturing toward our house. "We haven't much time."

The path is deserted. Our feet tap against the stones. A siren shrieks close by, warning that the curfew is coming.

We sprint after Mom down the alley to Sam's house.

"Do I have to go home?" asks Sam. "Can I come back to your house?"

"Not tonight," says Mom. "Your dad will be worried about you."

When we arrive, Sam's dad is sitting by the window, frowning. He points at us, leaving a mark on the glass with his finger.

I usually try to avoid Sam's dad; it's impossible to know how he's going to act.

He scratches his beard before heaving himself up and stumbling on his bad leg. He opens the door. The draft carries the smell of boiling goat meat.

"It's not Samdup's fault they're late," Mom says quickly. "Did you hear about the market today?"

He looks up at her. "I know what's been going on out there and we don't want any part of it."

I peer behind him into the house, spotting the piles of dirty pots and pans on the countertops.

Mom squeezes my shoulder.

Sam opens his mouth, then shrugs and steps inside. His eyes say everything.

Sam's dad thumps the door shut.

The last of the light is gone now. It's dark and we're breaking the curfew.

STORIES

Mom grips my hand and leads me briskly toward our house. I'm alert. My eyes flicker over shadows and my ears tune in to every rustle.

When we reach the front door Mom fumbles with the padlock and I keep it steady as she slides in the key. As soon as we're inside, Mom gathers our warm sweaters and throws them onto the bed in a pile. I breathe in the familiar scent of home. I bend down to take my shoes off.

"Leave them on until Dad gets home," she says.

"Are we going somewhere?" I ask.

Mom glances out the window. "I don't know yet."

Dad strides in minutes later, wrapped up in layers of woolen coats, and kisses Mom. He hugs me, his long hair falling from under his hat. His cold nose presses against my cheek. I smell the leathery tang of the animals.

"Listen to me," says Dad, taking my shoulders. "The whole village is going to be blamed for this. The Wujing will think we're all behind it. No more going off by yourself."

I notice the wrinkles on his forehead and around his eyes as I nod and sit down on the bench at the table.

Dad unhooks the rusty teapot hanging above the stove, slides his hand inside, and pulls out a bundle of yuan fastened with red string. The same kind the monks bless and give out as bracelets.

He snaps the string with a knife before reaching into his pocket and pulling out more notes. He peels back each corner and counts them, before dividing the money into three piles.

"I want you to hold on to this, my little yak," he says, handing me the biggest bundle. "In case anything happens. Hide it. Keep it safe."

I look to Mom. She smiles at me. I stand tall, shoulders back. "You can count on me." I stare

Dad straight in the eye so he knows I really mean it. It's the first time he's ever trusted me with something like this. I fold the money in half and hide it in my inside pocket. It's the most money I've ever held.

Dad sighs, then draws me and Mom toward him, scooping us under his arms. The fur from his coat is warm and soft. I lean my head against it and close my eyes. The Man on Fire glares back at me, surrounded by bright orange and screaming.

"What do we do?" whispers Mom.

"Carry on like normal," replies Dad, squeezing us before letting go. "Try not to draw attention to ourselves."

I nod slowly but stay rooted to the bench, grappling with Dad's words.

Dad drags his desk to the window and sits looking out. "Turn the light off," he says.

"You should eat something," Mom says to him, breaking up the dried yak's manure and feeding it to the kitchen fire.

"In a minute," he says. "I need to write first."

By day Dad works for the local newspaper. By night he writes leaflets for the secret resistance.

Mom lights a butter candle off the fire and places it on his desk.

The smoke stings my nostrils. The room

flickers, the flames reflecting in the tiny glass windows that keep out the drafts. Shadows dance on the wooden ceiling beams that Mom painted with swirling pictures of clouds, dragons, and snow lions.

"Eat," says Mom, passing me a plate of mutton momos.

My favorite. I dip one in the red chili sauce and bite into the dough. The juice spills down my fingers.

"Will the man be all right?" I ask quietly.

"He's in the hospital," says Mom.

"Who is he?"

"It's Mr. Tenzin," she replies. "The tailor."

"Why did he do it?" I ask, making patterns on my plate with the momo and sauce.

Mom is silent next to me.

"He wants change," says Dad, from his desk. "He wanted to tell the world how bad it is here."

"Enough," says Mom. She pulls another candle out of a drawer and lights it from the fire. "This is for him."

Throughout dinner there's nothing to mask my thoughts. I hear every chew of meat and scrape of chopsticks against plates.

"Can't you hum?" I ask Mom.

"It's not a night for humming," she replies.

I stand and run my fingers over the spines of my favorite books.

"Well, can you tell me a story?" I ask. "Like you used to?"

She clears the plates and sits next to me by the fire. Her face is lit up by the flames.

"Long ago, your grandfather was a nomad," she says. "He'd roam the grasslands with his yaks, churning buttermilk and collecting the wildflowers. Back then the land was filled with spruce trees, and colorful prayer flags hung between them, fluttering in the wind. Herds of wild deer grazed the grasses and birds filled the blue skies."

Dad reaches for Mom's hand and she smiles.

"What changed?" I ask, twisting my turquoise ring around my finger.

Mom passes me a yak's wool blanket and I cuddle up with it.

"There's never a good time for that story," says Dad.

Mom leans forward. "One day, the Chinese army invaded and herded the nomads in a way that they would never even do to their own animals. They forced them off the land. They ripped up the ground and dug deep into the earth to mine, scarring the landscape. The deer leapt away. The birds and the butterflies flew off."

Mom rearranges the red wool braided into her hair.

"Maybe that's enough," says Dad.

I can't take my eyes off the fire. With every flicker, my skin crawls.

There's a tap on the door.

Dad glances at us. His forehead creases.

Mom grabs my hand.

There's another tap.

"Get back," Dad says. He stands, knocking his chair over. It scrapes across the floor.

SECRETS

"It's me," whispers a voice. "Sam."

I look at Dad. Relief flashes across his face.

"Get in here, quick," says Dad, holding the door ajar. "What are you thinking, breaking the curfew like that? Did anyone see you?"

Sam shakes his head, sliding his shoes off. I realize I'm still wearing mine and slip them off too.

"You shouldn't have risked coming here," says Dad, his voice rising. "We talked about this, remember?"

"Shh," says Mom, ushering everyone away from the door. "Does your dad know you're here, Sam?"

"He's asleep." Sam shrugs. "He won't notice I'm gone."

"And the soldiers?" asks Dad.

"I've been watching the patrols go past all evening. I know when the breaks are." Sam looks up at my parents. "I'm sorry. I just wanted to know if there was any news."

"Are the soldiers still outside the monastery?" I ask.

Sam nods. "Do you think they'll surround the village too?" he asks Dad. "They must believe the monastery is involved with the man on fire. Why else would they be there?"

"You're probably right," says Dad.

Sam puffs up, proud that Dad agrees with him, and I'm instantly jealous.

Ever since Sam and I discovered that Dad is in the secret resistance, we've tried to prove that we should be allowed to join. Recently, it's as if Sam's been getting more things right than me.

I think of how Dad gave me the money to look after, and I relax.

"I'll make us some tea," Mom offers.

Dad tilts his head toward the kitchen.

"Come and give me a hand, Tash," says Mom.

"Not now," I moan. My mind swarms with questions.

"Tash?" says Mom, using her stern voice, so I know there's no arguing with her.

"I'll just be a second," I say to Sam. I form a fist with my right hand and stick out my little finger and thumb, before mimicking an eagle soaring with it. It's our secret signal, our promise that we'll always tell each other everything.

I cross our living space into the kitchen area.

"Here," I say, placing the butter churner next to Mom.

"Not so fast," she says as I turn to go.

I let the butter slide off the spoon and drop into the water while she stirs.

Dad ushers Sam to the window. Their voices lower.

I strain my ears but the cups clink and clank and the butter tea boils. I can't hear what they're saying.

Mom stirs slowly.

"I'll do it," I say, taking it from her and blending the mixture quickly.

"Promise me you won't break curfew like Sam," says Mom. "We're lucky to be here, you know. Stay quiet and remember the rules."

Mom's said it to me a million times before but there's something in her voice that makes me listen this time.

"I promise," I say.

When it's ready, I carry the steaming tea to Dad and Sam.

"Thanks," says Sam, taking his cup.

We sit in silence, huddled by the stove, sipping the warm broth and praying for the Man on Fire, until Dad insists on guiding Sam back to his house.

"See you tomorrow," says Sam.

I glare at him. I want to be the one sneaking around with Dad.

SOLDIERS

The next day at school they call an assembly. Our headmaster stands up and declares, "There will be no talk of the incident. Anyone found discussing it will be punished."

That's it. No mention of a man on fire. Nothing about the soldiers flooding into our village. Everyone is acting as if it never happened.

Sam catches up to me as we file silently out of the hall, in our separate lines, to the concrete grounds.

"The soldiers are still outside the monastery," he whispers.

"I know," I say. It was the first thing I checked when I woke up.

"Back in line!" yells a teacher.

"What did Dad say to you last night?" I ask.

Lhamo taps me. "Stop talking. You'll get us all punished."

I ignore her. "What did he say?"

"Nothing," says Sam. He takes my hand and squeezes it before turning back to his line.

✦ ✦ ✦

Dad's already home when I get back from school. He's not usually there before me. He paces in front of his desk with his fingers pressed against his forehead.

Spread over the table is a pile of green papers. They're instructions telling Dad exactly what he needs to write in the town newspaper. The authorities deliver them every week.

"What's happened?" I ask. "Is it the Man on Fire?"

"There's no news of him," says Mom.

"Then what's wrong?" I ask.

Mom and Dad glance at each other.

"I got the information I was waiting for today," Dad says. "Something I need to pass on."

"But that sounds good," I say.

"The village is under lockdown. No one and nothing is getting in or out without proper papers. I'll never get the message past the police."

Mom lays her arm around his shoulders.

"Where does the message have to go?" I ask.

"To the mountains," says Dad.

"Can't you get someone to sneak out?"

"They'd get caught," replies Mom, getting up to stoke the fire. "There are spies everywhere; it's too risky."

I nod, confused by it all.

"I know what will cheer us up," says Mom. "Come and help me, Tashi-la?"

She heaves a trunk from under her bed. I grab a corner and help carry it into the kitchen. It thumps down to the floor. I trace the carved wood with my fingertips.

"This is in honor of the man on fire," Mom says, unlatching the top.

I picture him running down the street and feel my body turn numb.

Dust escapes from the trunk, making me sneeze. It fills the air around the candles, shimmering.

Mom reaches in and cups a picture in her palm, a small portrait of the Dalai Lama. I remember the first time I saw the photograph of the smiling, round-faced man; he didn't look like a world leader to me. By then I was used to guns, uniforms, and hard stares.

"This is a different kind of power," Mom says, handing me the picture. "One that stems from love and not hate."

I tuck the photo into my pocket, feeling its thick paper.

She pulls out a dress. She's shown dresses like this to me before: her traditional clothes, her chubas.

"You can put it on," she says.

I slip the heavy material over my head. It hangs all the way to my feet. Mom fastens the sash around my waist.

Dad smiles at us. I spin around and around, butterflies gathering in my stomach. Last week a whole family got taken away for wearing chubas.

Mom takes my hair, divides it into sections, and braids it around my head. She sings a song about snow lions. The notes spiral through the room.

I join in, my voice rising in volume as we reach the chorus.

"We are the people of the mountains.
The mountain air runs through our veins."

Dad adds a high-tenor harmony.

*"We can breathe where others can't.
Mountain warriors of peace."*

Mom stops singing. "Not too loud, you two," she says, digging through the trunk. She lifts out a prayer bowl.

Lights outside cast shadows on the wall. I hear a clunk as a door is closed.

Dad peers out the window.

"What is it?" asks Mom.

I can make out the silhouettes of army trucks in front of Dolka's house. Soldiers fling her door open and light floods the darkness. They pour inside, ducking under the low wooden door.

8

RUN

"Why are they here?"

"It's the Wujing," Dad says. "They're searching the village."

"Why?" I ask. "What have we done?"

"They'll be looking for a reason to arrest people." Dad clenches his fist. "They need someone to blame."

I think of the illegal resistance leaflets hidden under the yak dung, the Dalai Lama's photograph in my pocket, the prayer bowl on the floor. Our house is full of reasons.

"I should have seen this coming," says Dad. "I expected it last night but not today."

Mom digs out the leaflets and stuffs them into the fire. The paper curls. Ashes blow about the room.

Dad throws a yak-hide backpack onto the floor and chucks the prayer bowl into it. He comes back from the bedroom with an armful of papers and shoves them into the fire.

I stand there, swaying, unsure of what to do.

"Watch the window," says Dad.

"Where are they now?" asks Mom.

I peek outside.

"Two houses away."

Mom drags the trunk back into the bedroom.

"Take off the chuba," she says, stopping to untie the sash. "Do you remember the way to the vulture tree?"

I nod, pulling my arms out of the dress.

"Go there and wait for us."

"Why can't you come?" I ask.

Dad stops in front of the window. "They're at Rin's," he says.

My heart races. We're next.

Dad riffles through a leaflet before sliding it into the backpack. He fastens the top and threads my arms through the straps.

"When you get out, run," he says. "Don't let anyone see you."

There's a thump on the door. Metal hits the wood.

I try to think what the Dalai Lama would do but I have no thoughts, only blood pumping through my body. Mom steers me toward the back window. She unbolts the wooden shutters and pushes the glass. Cold air rushes inside.

Mom strokes my hair. "Remember the vulture tree. I'll meet you there."

"Keep the bag safe," says Dad. "It's important."

I glance back and forth from Mom to Dad, unable to process what's happening.

"I know you can do it," Dad says, kissing my forehead. "You have the luck of the dragon."

"And the bravery of the snow lion," whispers Mom.

There's a bang.

The house shudders. Dad jumps in front of me and Mom, making a wall between us and the door.

"Go," he whispers.

Another bang. The wood cracks.

Mom hoists me up.

"Come with me," I say, squeezing my shoulders through the window. The splinters snag my skin.

"I can't," Mom says. "Now run."

She pushes my feet and I tumble down the other side.

SKIRT

I crouch so that my eyes are above the window-sill. I have a clear view of the kitchen and living space. Dad's by the front door.

Where's Mom?

I scan the kitchen, past the table, the cupboards, the fireplace. She's not there. I look through to the bedroom. There's a flash of red skirt caught in the cupboard door. She's hiding.

"Your skirt," I whisper, praying that she realizes it's trapped in the door.

"Dad, Mom's skirt!" I wave at him.

He motions for me to get away.

The front door flies open, banging against the wall.

Six soldiers storm into the room: Spaniel, Wildface, Dagger, and three others I don't recognize, in olive-colored uniforms. The Wujing. Guns hang from their belts. They grab Dad's arms. The commander stands in front of him.

I duck down.

"Where are the papers?" he spits.

"I don't know what you're talking about." Dad's voice wavers.

There's a thump.

"Where are the leaflets?" the commander asks again.

Silence.

"Search the place!" yells the commander.

"Yes, sir," reply the police.

In my hands is everything they're looking for. I should run, hide the bag, bury the photograph.

I can't leave Mom.

I hear the clanking of objects being knocked over, the slide of drawers opening, and the smash of things breaking.

"Search the other rooms," says the commander.

"No," I whisper.

Footsteps head farther away.

I peek over the windowsill.

The soldiers tear through to the bedroom, closer to the cupboard and Mom's red skirt.

"I told you there's nothing here," says Dad.

Spaniel grabs Dad's hair, forcing his arms tighter behind his back.

My stomach crunches. I dig my nails into the wooden windowsill.

I catch glimpses of Dad's face. I need to see his eyes—calm, steady, and all-knowing—but as I meet his gaze they're wild and bloodshot.

I know that everything's gone wrong.

Go, he mouths at me.

The commander whips his head around, following Dad's line of sight.

"At the window," he cries. "Get her!"

YAKS

I lunge forward, scrambling on the dirt. My knees scrape against the stones. I pull myself to my feet and run.

"Stop!" a soldier shouts. "Stop right there!"

My skirt restricts my legs as I sprint. I yank it up over my knees. The bag thumps against my side. I can't see through the thick darkness.

Footsteps pound behind me.

My wool slippers are soft on the hard ground. Every stone pierces my foot.

I turn a corner and I'm at Sam's house. I fight the urge to run inside. The soldiers are close and I can't put his family in danger.

I tear onward, leaping over a ditch and ducking past our neighbors' houses.

My braid unwraps from around my head and whips against my back.

On the main road a patrol truck rumbles. Another follows. I see the yellow lights, heading toward my house. The Wujing are coming. I have to get away from the village.

I make it past the houses, toward the yak stables. I glance behind me. There's no one there. I slip inside a yak shed.

It's warm indoors and smells of manure and damp. Mani's yak, Eve, lies on a thin layer of straw. She takes up almost all the space in the barn.

I hear the clunk of boots.

A stitch burns my side. I rest my arm on the yak to balance. I can't keep running. I squeeze around Eve, touching her wet nose. My whole hand fits over the top of her nostrils. She breathes out and her earthy breath warms my fingers.

Lying down, I edge closer to the side of her body, lift her fleecy long hair, and slide underneath her coat. I'm just about hidden by an oily, soft blanket. I squeeze my eyes shut and will the soldiers to keep walking.

The footsteps get louder. I cling to Eve, allowing her fur to cover me completely. Nuzzling my forehead against her body, I smell her grassy skin. Her heart beats slow and steady.

"We can't have lost her," a voice says outside.

"She'll be in one of these stables."

Please don't come in here.

Light beams into the shed and hits the wall above me. I peer through Eve's hair. The soldiers shine the flashlights on the yak, casting long shadows up the wall.

"Check in the straw," one of the soldiers says.

It's Spaniel.

Eve lifts her right leg. The flashlights spotlight it.

Any hope I had drains from my body. As soon as Eve stands they'll see me.

The soldiers aim their flashlights at Eve's head and I remain in darkness, under her thick fur. The strands tickle my neck.

A soldier steps closer and Eve snorts at him. He shuffles forward.

Eve heaves herself up, sending straw and woolly hair flying. She lunges her head, catching his side with her huge horns.

The soldier growls and takes a step back.

I hold my breath. I can see his feet on the other side of Eve. Drops of sweat gather on my forehead.

The soldier bends down and plunges his hand

into the straw. His head is blocked from my sight by the fur hanging from Eve's belly.

I close my eyes, praying that he can't see me.

Eve throws her head to the side, more forcefully this time, jabbing the soldier with her horns.

"Argh!" yells the soldier, grabbing hold of his back. He unhooks his gun. I hear him cock it but I can't see where it's pointing.

Please, not Eve.

A second pair of legs arrives. "Calm down. There's nothing here."

Eve scrapes her hoof against the floor and lowers her horns. She cries a long, low grunt. The noise makes the air quiver.

"What are you waiting for?" asks Spaniel. "Search the other stables."

From the shed next to me, another yak cries.

A third bellows from farther away.

Eve nudges her horns forward and calls again.

"Come on," says one of the soldiers. "Let's get out of here."

The flashlight beams drop and my heart starts beating again. I pull my knees into my chest and hug them until I can't hear any noise. I find the wall with my hand and use it to pull myself up.

I turn to Eve and stroke her neck.

"Thank you," I whisper.

VULTURE

I stand at the edge of the path and look out into the night. I have to cut across the grasslands to get to the vulture tree. I'll be exposed, with no houses or trees for cover. I know Mom would warn me about the wild wolves and leopards, but now is not the time to follow the rules.

I have to meet Mom.

I tighten the bag around my back. The tree is in the distance, rising high above the bushes. I see the dark shapes of two huge vultures in the branches. As I get closer they flap their wings, annoyed at being disturbed, before settling back down to watch me with their beady eyeballs.

"Mom?" I whisper.

There's no reply. My stomach turns. I was hoping she would already be here.

I look into the black fields.

Did anyone see me?

I don't feel safe on the ground. I bend my knees and jump as high as I can. My fingers close around a branch and for a moment I hang there before heaving my other hand up. I've climbed up here a million times with Sam. I can do it by myself.

I walk my feet up the trunk and maneuver them over a branch. I shuffle along until I'm leaning back into the trunk.

From up here I can see the dimly lit windows in town. I stay as still as I can, straining my ears for the whoosh of movement through the grass.

In the distance, military truck lights snake up the road. Above me, a vulture gives its rasping cry. The last time I was here, Sam whistled the vulture call and they flew to him.

"Sam?" I whisper hopefully. "Was that you?"

There's no reply.

I hold the Dalai Lama photo and hug the bag, wondering how many laws I'm breaking. I unbutton the top of the backpack and pull the leather bag open. My fingers close around a prayer bowl. I move it aside and my hand brushes against papers. I lift them out and gather them in my hands. *The Snow Lion.* Dad's secret leaflet for the resistance. I can just about make out the headings: **NEWS** and **TEACHINGS.** It's too dark to read the rest.

My attention drifts. There is so much I don't know about *The Snow Lion* and the risks my dad has taken.

Three years ago, he burst into the house, his face twisted with worry. "Hundreds of monks are holding a protest in Lhasa."

"How?" asked Mom. "What are they doing?"

"Sitting peacefully," replied Dad. I pictured rows of monks in their maroon robes among the concrete streets of the city.

"But they've been called a threat to social stability."

Dad beckoned us to follow him. He led us to Sam's house, where we gathered around the TV and watched the World News channel. We didn't have electricity often, but when we did, they had the clearest signal.

I tapped my foot as we waited.

After what seemed like forever the reporter said, "Demonstrations in the capital city of Lhasa . . ."

And then the screen went black, sucking all the color and sound with it.

Sam's dad knelt on his hands and knees and fiddled with the wires.

Dad flicked back and forth through the channels. The others were still working.

"Come on . . ." he muttered.

The World News channel flashed back.

"There," said Mom.

We watched the screen but there was no mention of Lhasa or the monks. The reporter had already moved on to a different story.

"Someone has to tell the real news around here," said Sam's mom quietly.

"Maybe there's something I can do," said Dad. "They'll never suspect me."

"We could use the secret resistance to find out what's really happening," said Sam's dad.

Dad nodded slowly.

I thought Mom would be worried, but she took his face in her hands and said, "I'm proud of you."

From then on Dad used the leaflets to write the truth. Our truth.

I chew my cracked lip as I remember. My throat is raw, craving water. I must have been here for hours. I think of the Dalai Lama and how he can sit in the same position meditating for hours. The longest I've been able to do it is for thirteen minutes.

There's still no sign of Mom. I twist my turquoise ring back and forth nervously. *What if she needs my help?*

I think about tying my sweater to a branch but it's too cold. I feel for my middle finger and slide off my ring. When Mom gave it to me she wrapped red string around the metal to make it fit. I bite a strand with my teeth, unravel it quickly, and tie it to a branch. The ring dangles, swinging back and forth in the breeze. The silver glints in the moonlight.

She couldn't miss it.

RANSACK

The first thing I notice is the door, hanging by one hinge.

My hands tremble as I push it and duck inside. I can faintly smell smoke from the fire as I drop my backpack to the ground.

"Mom?" I whisper, pushing past the knocked-over bench and rushing to the cupboard where she hid. My fingers close around the metal handle and I tug it open.

It's empty.

"Dad," I say. "Are you in here?"

There's no answer.

I reach into my drawer, hoping to find our yak bell. I feel around the corners. It's gone.

I check under the bed. They have to be here somewhere.

I hunt for matches and a butter candle. My fingers close around one and I light it with shaky hands. I spot Mom's fleece scarf, half buried in a pile of blank papers and Dad's writing pens. It's ripped and torn but still soft and it smells of fresh dough, just like she does.

Where are they?

The door creaks on its hinge. The soldiers must have come back for me. I blow out the candle, spilling the hot wax down my hand.

There's a crunch: a shoe crushing glass underneath it.

The footsteps get closer.

"Tash? You here?"

"Sam?" I ask, lifting my head.

"Tash!" Sam runs over and kneels next to me. "Are you hurt?" He shines a flashlight in my eyes.

I let out my breath. Sam is the only one I can trust now. Seeing him reminds me that I'm not alone.

He grabs my hand and squeezes it tightly in his.

"They're gone," I say, blinking.

"I saw the army push them into the truck," he says. "I thought they had you too."

"I ran away. I shouldn't have left them."

"They would have wanted you to get away," he says.

I remember the photograph of the Dalai Lama. I slip my fingers into my pocket and feel it filling me with strength. I pull it out and stare at his happy face.

I have to do something to help.

Think, Tash. Think.

The Dalai Lama stares back at me. If there's one person who would know what to do, it's him.

He's my glimmer of hope.

"I'm going to India," I say.

"What?" asks Sam.

"I'm going to India to see the Dalai Lama," I say, passing the photograph to him.

"What can he do?" Sam rubs the picture with his thumb.

"He's the leader of Tibet," I say. "He has to help."

"He hasn't been here for fifty years. He won't be able to do anything from India."

"Please," I say. "I can feel it. If we can just make it to him, he'll get them out."

Sam nods slowly. It's too dark for me to read his face. "I've heard of people walking to India before," he says, "but it takes weeks, maybe months."

"That's too long!"

I know the stories. People starve to death in prison. They mysteriously disappear. I can't think about what might happen to Mom and Dad. The longer they're there, the less chance there is of getting them out.

"We can't stay here," I say. The soldiers will be back.

"Gather anything we might need," whispers Sam. "It will be a long journey."

I want to reach out and hug him.

Sam's coming with me.

"Get food, water, clothes, and as much yak dung as we can carry to use as fuel," he continues. He tosses a disc of dry yak dung down at me. "I need to get my things."

"Can your dad help us?" I ask, gathering the discs. A few have crumbled in the fall but most are dry and solid.

"Dad would never make the journey with his leg."

I nod. I knew that already.

"And he'd probably stop us from going."

"What are you going to tell him?" I ask.

Sam shrugs. "I'll be straight back."

He dashes out and along the path. I'm left, wishing he was still here.

The blackness shifts; it's getting lighter. We have to be quick.

I scoop the tsampa grains back into the metal jars and shake the sheepskin coats out. I toss useless items over my shoulder, keeping warm clothes and cooking supplies in a pile in front of me. The cooking pots are all heavy. I choose the lightest one.

Soon I have a mound of provisions: water bottles, tsampa, one cooking pot, two spoons, one knife, all the discs of dried yak dung, rope, empty burlap sacks, the sheet of tarpaulin Dad used to fix the leak in the roof, sleeping bags, blankets, winter coats, and matches.

My skin tingles. We have to get out of here before someone spots us. I pull on my thickest socks and dig out my snow boots from the bottom of a trunk. I haven't tried them on since last year and squeeze them onto my feet, feeling the soft wool lining. I stand and feel taller.

There's just enough space in my backpack for my gloves. I slide on Dad's sheepskin coat. It's big and bulky. I tuck the Dalai Lama photograph into my inside pocket and wrap Mom's ripped scarf around my neck. I'm ready.

I bundle the supplies into two of the sacks and fasten them with rope.

I stand back. They're big. It's a lot to carry.

I strap Dad's backpack to my front and heave a bundle onto my back. The weight pushes down against my chest.

Sam appears at the doorway, wearing layers of sweaters and a sheep's wool hat. I let out a sigh of relief.

"What did your dad say?"

"Nothing," replies Sam. "He won't even notice I'm gone."

I study Sam's face. He averts his eyes and for the first time I can see how much he looks like his father.

"Let's go," he says, heaving a bundle onto his back.

I push the creaking door aside and step through the frame.

CURFEW

The air is still and cold. Patrol trucks rumble in the distance. The curfew will be lifted soon.

"Hurry up, Tash," says Sam.

I'm moving as fast as I can. The bag's weight is slowing me down, squashing my chest and shooting pain down my lower back. There's nothing I can throw away. Dad always says that the mountains are harsh and unkind to those who aren't prepared.

We creep down the street to Kalsang's door. His family owns a truck. They could take us to the mountains. It's parked right next to their house so as not to block the narrow road. I squeeze around the hood and knock gently on the rough wood. Inside is a dim light. I close my hands around my eyes and peek through the gap in the blind. I see a rug and a chair next to a carved table. On it sits a steaming mug of tea.

Someone is awake.

I knock on the window and wait.

The curtain twitches. I knock again. Twice.

Sam flinches at every sound.

Why aren't they opening the door?

"Let's try the next one," Sam says.

I realize what he's thinking. They don't want to help us. Not after what happened last night.

At the next house I hear the scraping of a chair being pushed back. I try a different approach.

"It's me," I whisper. "Tashi."

Sam bounces up and down beside me to keep warm.

The door stays shut.

I turn the handle and rattle it.

"Please," I say.

"Stop," says Sam, scanning the path. "You're going to get us caught."

I slam the palm of my hand against the door.

"Let's try someone else," Sam says. He rests his hand on my shoulder. "They'd be risking everything to help us."

I clench my fist, wishing I could pound it against the door.

"Wait," says Sam. "I have an idea. Dorjee's sister lives over there, on the corner."

I glance at the small house. There's smoke rising from the chimney and I can tell it has been recently whitewashed. A bird perches next to it and sings its dawn call.

"There'll be a patrol coming through soon," says Sam, beckoning me forward.

I run to the house and tap with one finger on her door. It opens an inch.

"Who's there?" asks a hoarse voice.

"It's Tashi," I whisper. "Please let me in."

The latch clicks and Dorjee's sister ushers us inside.

"Who's this?" she asks, pointing at Sam.

"I'm Sam," he says. "I know your brother."

She studies him for a second before nodding.

"You need to get as far away from here as possible," she says. "If the police find you, they'll never let you go." She rips a piece of thick paper and scribbles a note on it. "Take this to the tent shop in the main square. My brother will give you what you need."

I glance outside. It's almost light. The market will be opening.

"Thanks," I say, heading for the door. Maybe we can catch him while he sets up the shop, before the soldiers get there.

"You can't go looking like that," she says. "They're searching for you." She shuffles off and returns with scissors. Clasping my long hair, she snips it off in two strokes so it's the same length as Sam's. I run my fingers through the strands. My throat is scratchy and I try to swallow it away. All I can think about is Mom braiding my hair last night.

Dorjee's sister gathers what's left of my hair and ties it up on top of my head.

"This was my husband's," she says, sliding a woolly hat over my head before pulling the earflaps down. "Now you two could be brothers."

She passes me the note. "Go, quickly. Curfew's over and it's not safe for you here."

PACT

Sam fastens the bag tighter around my shoulders. It sits higher on my hips now, so I'm able to keep up with him.

"What about here?" asks Sam, nodding toward a wooden chicken shed.

We stash our big bags behind it. I hesitate over the backpack. It's too risky to take it into the market. I stuff it underneath the shed, burying it beneath straw. Hens follow me in a line onto the stone path and I usher them back toward the shed.

Sam beckons me and I peer around the side of the alley into the main square. Soldiers guard every side like statues. It's the first time I've been back since the day the man set himself on fire. I reach out and grip Sam's coat to steady myself.

I cast my eyes over each of the soldiers to check that Spaniel, Wildface, and Dagger aren't there.

There's a trick that Dad taught me, a way to tell if a soldier is looking for trouble or will leave you alone. You study the way each one stands. If they're slumping, or leaning slightly, you're safe. The first sign of trouble is a fidget. It can be a toe tap or a finger twitch. The second clue is the eyes.

"Ready?" asks Sam.

The soldiers all look sleepy.

I pull my hat down as far as it will go. "Ready."

Their eyes follow us as we enter. The main square looks empty. It only takes me a second to realize why. The corrugated metal doors of the shop fronts are rolled down. There are no stalls spilling onto the street selling brightly colored cloth, kitchen utensils, and vegetables. All the shops are closed. On one of the doors is a poster saying DISOBEDIENCE WILL NOT BE TOLERATED. I wonder if Dorjee was arrested too. I scrunch the note in my fist.

"Let's pretend we're with those two." Sam nods toward a man with a spiky haircut and an older man, deep in discussion.

They're wearing black coats with multicolored pockets. They're not from around here. We sidle up and stand beside them. I do my best to look like a bored child.

"We should have got more supplies when we had the chance," says the older one.

"We'll stop before Lhasa," replies the other.

They're leaving the village. This could be our escape. I stare at Sam, trying to get his attention. *Lhasa*, I mouth.

Sam glances at the soldiers, then back at the men.

"Take us to Lhasa with you," I whisper. "We have money."

They gather around us, blocking us from the soldiers' view. It makes me nervous. "Please," I say. "You have to help us."

"How much have you got?"

I unzip my pocket and unfold the bundle of notes. The younger one snatches it out of my hand and counts it.

"Hey," I say, lunging at him. "That's mine."

He pulls his fingers out of reach. His hand is covered in splotches of paint.

"Give that back," says Sam.

"What are you going to do about it? Call the soldiers?"

I can't tear my eyes from the money in his hand.

"You have to take us with you," I hiss. "Otherwise you're nothing but a thief."

"Do you have papers?" asks the older man.

I shake my head.

"We'll never get you past the checkpoints on the road out of town. If you meet us farther down, where the grasslands cross the road, you can come."

I think about our secret way into the grasslands and hope it's still there. Sam and I discovered it last year when we followed a rabbit between two big rocks. A smaller boulder had fallen and broken the fence. The other rocks hid the damage.

I peer through the gap at the nearest soldier. He's tapping his foot. There aren't many people left in the square. We're going to miss our chance.

"How do we know you'll be there?" asks Sam.

The older man shrugs. "We'll be by the grasslands at midnight tomorrow. If you're there, you can come."

"We will be," I say. "Wait for us."

PATROL

Sam shakes his head. "We shouldn't have done that," he mutters. "We could have been seen. They might report us. There's probably a reward for turning us in."

I can't get distracted. The shock and numbness has started to fade and it's left me with a rage that shoots up and down my body. This is the only idea we have. Somehow, I'll make it work.

"It's at least a day of walking," I say. "We need to leave right now."

We get back to our bags, which are just as big as I remember, two huge sacks propped up behind the chicken shed. I lie down on my stomach to slide the backpack out.

"There must be something important in the backpack," I say.

"What's inside?" Sam asks.

"Dad's leaflet," I reply.

His eyes light up. He's on his hands and knees next to me, pulling at the buttons on the backpack. It unfastens and he lifts out the papers and flips through them. "You could have missed something."

"Let me see," I say, brushing straw from the outside of the backpack.

"In a minute," he says. "Maybe there's something that could help." His eyes scan the pages of the leaflet, as if he knows what he's looking for.

I snatch at the papers. I'm sick of Sam thinking he knows more than me.

"Dad gave them to me," I say. "Not you."

The words tumble out before I can stop them.

Sam's eyes flicker around us. He raises a finger to his lips. It maddens me even more.

Through the ground I feel a pulsing march. A patrol is near. I seize the papers and clutch them under my coat.

Sam flattens himself against the ground, hiding the backpack underneath him.

I drag my elbows across the earth and peek out under the shed. Three pairs of military boots stomp down in front of us. Stones ping in different directions. Behind them follows another row of soldiers.

I hear Sam's quick breathing next to me. He stares straight ahead.

My stomach twinges with guilt. It's not Sam's fault my parents are gone.

The last row of soldiers passes, and we lie and wait until they're far enough away. I watch a spider rotating in its web from the vibrations.

"Sam," I say finally. "I didn't mean that . . ."

"Forget it," he says. "Let's get out of here."

He jumps up and heaves the bag onto his back. He helps me with mine, tightening the rope. I smile at him but he won't look me in the eye, so I let the corners of my mouth drop; there's nothing to smile about right now anyway.

We move silently through the alleys, away from the patrol. My shoulders and neck ache from the weight. We pass the yak stables. Eve sticks her head over the half-door. She watches me with her dark eyes and sniffs with her big nostrils. Her pupils are wide; she knows something is wrong. I wish I could take her with me.

I turn to Sam. "Maybe we can borrow Eve?"

"We can't just take her," he says. "Mani needs her."

"He won't mind," I say, pausing to catch my breath for a second. "I used to help him with the herd when I was younger. He trusts me."

I stroke Eve's muzzle and unlatch the door. My breathing is loud and rasping. I can't seem to silence it.

What are you doing? mouths Sam.

I beckon him to follow me.

He shakes his head.

I push the shed door open with my side and let the bag thud to the floor. My skin is hot and sweating. Eve nuzzles me with her wet nose. Yaks are clever and loyal. When I was younger I'd help herd them after school. Dad wanted me to learn about the yaks. He wanted me to learn about everything.

I press my head against her thick coat, smelling the earthy dung and straw and holding her nose with my hands.

"Don't worry," I say to her.

She pushes against my hand.

"This is a bad idea," whispers Sam. "Come on."

"We have to take Eve," I say.

"Fine," says Sam, throwing his bag down. "But let's do this quickly."

A strange tingle creeps up my spine. A shadow is cast from the doorway. Mani, leaning on his staff, prayer beads swinging from his wrist, is watching us from the entrance.

DRAGON

Mani is swamped in a sheepskin coat; the sleeves run down past his hands. I'd forgotten how old he is. Mom says he's looked the same for as long as she can remember. Like the mountains, the wind is carved into his face.

I wonder how long he's been there. He doesn't say anything at first but pulls on the coral earring hanging from his right ear, stretching it and letting it ping back.

"What are you doing?" he asks eventually.

I don't know what to say or where to begin.

Mani shakes his head.

"Let's see what your parents have to say about

this," he says. "Or maybe I should call the police?"

"Wait," I say, fumbling in my pocket. "The soldiers took my parents and we need to get help." I pull out the photo of the Dalai Lama and pass it to him.

Mani stares down at the picture.

"You two could be in serious trouble for this," he says.

I notice an old yak bell hanging around his neck. It's rusty, with a wide slit at the bottom. I wish I had mine. They're special, carrying the spirit of the yak herders with them.

"You're going to find the Dalai Lama?" Mani asks.

I nod.

"I've always wanted to meet him," he says. "It's too late for me now."

Mani looks around. There's no sign of people anywhere. He leans on his staff, unbuttoning his jacket and opening one half of it. There, hemmed into the lining, is the same photograph.

"If you meet him, think of me," says Mani. "I've always wished to carry his blessing."

"Of course," I say.

"You can go," he whispers, "but look after my Eve. She's very precious."

"Thank you," I say, pressing my palms together.

"Go," says Mani, waving his staff. "Quickly."

I take the harness off the wall and slide it over Eve's back. She turns her head and nuzzles my side. Together, Sam and I heave the bags on and tie them with the rope. Sam leans on them with his body weight while I secure them. Eve follows me outside and I slip the rein over the tether post.

Mani appears from the next stable, leading a black yak with white markings over his eyes. The yak's thick hair and shaggy tail look like a skirt. His hooves stick out underneath it.

"This is Bones," says Mani, offering the lead to Sam. "They don't like to be separated."

Sam smiles and climbs onto Bones.

I put my foot on one of the bag holdings and swing my leg over Eve.

"Good luck with the journey," Mani says. "The yaks will keep you safe."

He gathers his lips together and gives a high-pitched whistle. The yaks respond instantly, propelled forward as if they've been slapped.

Sam points at the sky. For the first time in ages, there are clouds above the mountains. They glow red and pink with the morning sun. Two clouds have joined together to form a dragon's head, mouth open, two teeth pointing down. The wisps of cloud are the flames licking the sun. I hold my head up high and think of Dad.

I have the luck of the sky dragon.

JOURNEY

Eve steps into a ditch and I slide forward, slamming into the hump above her shoulders.

"Sorry, Eve," I mutter, shuffling back to find my balance.

Being a yak rider should run in my blood but my leg muscles ache from clinging on so tightly.

We approach the thick wire fence that surrounds the village. Two rocks stand to our right like giant guards.

Please let it be clear.

Sam dismounts. He moves slowly toward them, crushing the gravel under his boots.

"There's no one here!" he shouts.

"Is the fence still broken?" I ask.

He nods and disappears between the rocks with Bones.

I follow him. The rusty fence has bowed to the ground where the boulder fell and flattened it. The space between the rocks is just big enough to squeeze Eve through, though I have to tug at her harness to get her to move. As I step over the fence, my heart jumps.

We're escaping.

I spot Sam looking at the vast empty grasslands, walled in on all sides by the barren foothills. Bones makes a beeline for the path and Sam tugs him away, back into the overgrown grass.

We have to reach the rocky hill in the distance. I calculate it will take us about six more hours to arrive. Beyond the hill, the huge mountains rise out of the ground, gray and dappled with bright white snow. I've never felt so small.

"Did you see the police take anyone else away?" I ask Sam.

He shakes his head. "I know the man on fire had family in town, though. They'll lock up anyone connected with him."

"I wish he hadn't done it," I whisper. "There's no one to help us."

"Don't you see, Tash? That's why he did it.

Who's going to stand up for us? How do we get our voices heard?"

I glance backward. The houses are tiny dots on the horizon. My parents are still close by. I picture them huddled in a dark cell.

I only know one person who returned from prison. If the Wujing think Dad was involved with the Man on Fire they'll never let him out, and there's even less chance if they know about the leaflets.

Sam stares at the ridge jutting out of the mountain and the white steps that spiral up there. His gaze is distant and I know why. It's the place of the sky burials, and the last time we traveled there was for his mom.

Bones stops in front of me.

"What is it?" I ask.

Sam nods toward a group of farmers heading across the fields.

"Come here," he says, jumping off Bones.

He fastens my coat all the way up so that just my nose and eyes stick out. I breathe in the earthy scent of Dad.

"You really could be my brother." Sam smiles.

"Wandering nomads." I grin back. I realize it's not even a lie. I have no home now.

"If anyone asks," says Sam, "we're just taking these yaks to our father."

We ride on in silence. The yaks' hooves thud on the grass.

Eyes forward. Sit up straight. Most important, don't slide off.

The farmers are on their hands and knees, slicing the grass with their scythes. They don't even look up at us. We pass them and I feel a flutter of victory.

Hours go by and the sun shines from its highest point.

With each person we pass, I grow in confidence.

Until I see them.

LETTER

A line of uniformed soldiers sweeps across the fields in the distance. Farmers scramble out of their way. My heart beats faster.

"Sam," I say, pulling up alongside him. "Look."

The panic on his face tells me he's seen them.

He slides off, grabs Eve's rein, and tugs us toward a line of bushes marking a field border. Bones's thick horns stick out over the top of them.

"Lie down," Sam hisses at him.

Bones lowers his head and munches on the grass.

"As long as he keeps eating, they won't be able to see him," I say.

Sam presses his face against the hedge.

"Your dad always said that if anything like this happened, they'd tighten the military and put the whole area under lockdown. No one is allowed to move in or out."

I frown at Sam.

"We'll have to wait until it gets dark," he continues.

"We can't risk wasting any time," I say, watching the soldiers march forward. "The men with the truck will be waiting for us."

"Tash," Sam says quietly. "You're wanted by these people. If you go out there they'll question you. They'll find out who you are."

I sit on the ground, wishing that I could sneak past the soldiers and hating the idea of waiting.

Eve and Bones stop eating and look up at me.

I take the bag off my back and tear it open. The prayer bowl clatters to the ground. I think back to the night the soldiers came. Dad told me to keep the backpack safe.

There must be something important in there.

The copy of *The Snow Lion* lies crumpled at the bottom. I gather it in my hands and scan the pages.

A piece of paper falls onto my lap.

It's a letter. In each corner is a drawing of a quarter-moon.

Dear old friend,
How are the yaks? If you need some more I will be passing soon. Hopefully we will fly through the mountains and not stumble on the high passes and snow like the last time. My herd is currently 11 strong.
See you in December, or November at the earliest.
Yours,
Rinchen

A praying mantis lands on the top right corner of the page. I blow him off.

"We will get there," says Sam, eyes glued to the hedge.

I keep searching, brushing the letter aside and digging in the bag. There's nothing else in there.

I slide my hand inside and feel around the hem. Maybe there's something hidden in the seam.

Empty.

It's too much to take in. My head is spinning. I snap strands of grass between my fingers, each piece marking a countdown of the seconds.

I want to be on the move.

"The soldiers are getting close," says Sam. "Hide."

I dive toward the bottom of the hedge. The ground is damp and cold. Bugs move along the soil all around me.

Sam keeps a lookout through the bush branches. Bones finishes eating and lifts his head. I grab a handful of grass, holding it out to him.

"Come on," I whisper. "Eat it."

Bones eyes it for a second before lowering his head and munching the grass out of my hand. Bits stick out the sides of his leathery mouth. I pray it was quick enough and the soldiers didn't spot his horns over the hedge. I turn and peer through the branches.

The soldiers swish past the long grass, poking at the bush with their sharp bayonets.

Bones shakes his head.

"What was that?" asks a soldier.

"I heard something too," says another.

I throw my hand out to Bones.

Don't stick your head up now.

The soldiers edge closer, slicing the leaves in half with their knives. My heart beats so hard I'm sure they must hear it.

A bayonet sticks straight through the hedge,

coming out right above me. Its blade glints in the light, catching the sun.

Ten centimeters lower and it would have speared me. I lean away from the hedge. Sam shuffles backward.

"There's something there," says a soldier. "I heard it."

The hedge rustles. A pheasant squawks and flies out next to us and up into the sky, its long tail flicking behind it.

"It was just a stupid bird."

"Come on. We've got enough land to cover today."

I place my hands flat on the ground and gasp shallow breaths.

Sam shakes his head. "That was far too close."

I nod. "What will happen when they reach our village?"

"I don't want to know," says Sam.

"He'll be all right," I say, squeezing his hand. "Your dad, I mean."

But I don't know that. I don't know anything for sure.

GRASSLANDS

At dusk the crickets chirp and the fireflies dance. The fields become a lake of twinkling lights.

Eve and Bones are lying down with their heads resting on each other.

"Come on, Eve," I say. "Time to go."

She opens her brown eyes and looks up at me. I rest my forehead against her coarse hair. She grunts. I know she thinks I'm mad but she lifts her feet and stands. Sam and I climb onto the yaks and set off, one step closer to finding the Dalai Lama and saving my parents.

Above us, the stars shine brightly.

"We live on the roof of the world," says Sam.

Mom always says that you couldn't get much closer to the stars than this. When India collided with the rest of Asia the mountains were pushed up out of the earth toward the sky.

I'm thankful to be on Eve, above the grasses swirling with humming bugs and snakes.

"I thought there'd be something important in the backpack," I say. "But there's only the leaflet and that letter."

"What letter?" asks Sam. "Let me see." He slows Bones and we stop. He shines his flashlight through his fingers to limit the brightness and stares at the writing.

"Dad's name isn't Rinchen," I say, confused by the signature at the end. "It's Sonam."

"This isn't a letter, Tash," whispers Sam. "It's a secret message."

My breath catches.

"How do you know?" I ask.

"It must be. It's not addressed to anyone. Why else would your dad have it?"

"I knew there was something important in the bag," I say, trying to keep my voice down. My stomach flutters. "Dad told me there was some information he was trying to pass on. I bet this is it."

"Now we just have to crack it." Sam grins.

We hurry onward through the darkness, stopping along the way to steal glances at the letter with the flashlights.

After what seems like forever, I recognize the big rock jutting out of the ground. It marks the place where the grasslands cross the road.

"We're almost there," I whisper.

I spot the dark shape of a truck, parked offroad. Specks of light shine through the cracks in the back door.

Maybe it's a trap?

I slide off Eve and tiptoe silently toward the truck, leading her behind me.

Sam switches the flashlight on and off as a signal.

I hear the click of a door opening and footsteps as a figure paces toward us.

A flashlight beam shines in my face and I shield my eyes, unable to see who it is.

"You're lucky," says the man. His husky voice tells me it's the older one. "We were just about to give up and leave."

"We weren't certain you'd be here," says Sam.

"I gave you my word," he says. "That's important in times like this."

My mind spins with thoughts of money. We have to get in the truck before they discover that we don't have any more.

Sam switches his flashlight on too. The man's mustache is outlined in the shadows.

"I'm Jinpa," he says, holding his hand out.

"There were soldiers back there," I say hurriedly. "We should go."

We follow him to a beat-up green truck, parked on a slant, with two wheels on the road and two up the hill. The younger man from the square leans against the passenger door, watching us.

Jinpa tugs the creaking back door open. It forms a ramp. Inside, it's bigger than I expect and the back is filled with giant masks, materials, and costumes that hang from the ceiling. It smells of dust and mothballs.

I notice a woman sitting on round cushions on the floor. She has short, scruffy hair and soft cheeks.

"What are you doing with the yaks?" asks Jinpa. "Your best bet is to set them free and point them toward home."

"No," Sam and I say in unison.

"We need them for our journey," I add.

"We promised to look after them," Sam explains.

I smile at him.

Jinpa stares at the yaks. "They can't come."

"I'll watch them," the woman says, standing up and climbing out. "They won't be any trouble."

Jinpa looks too tired to argue. He shrugs his shoulders.

"Get them inside," he says.

I nod and pray the truck can fit us all in.

Moonlight shines into the back, reflecting off the metal walls. I walk up the ramp, leading Eve. She takes one step up and stops. I tug at her gently. She tosses her head from side to side and tries to turn around. The lead slips out of my hand and she backs away.

"Let's try Bones," says Sam quickly, leading him up to the truck.

This time I stand behind Bones and push his back.

"He's not budging." I lean my body weight against him.

I try again to get Eve inside the truck but she increases her protests, stamping her front hoof, eyes wide and nostrils flared.

"You'll have to leave without them," says Jinpa.

I think of Mani. The journey across the mountains seems impossible without the yaks.

I sink back against the truck side.

"We're not waiting any longer," hisses Jinpa.

"You have to," I say. "I'm not leaving without the yaks."

Jinpa sighs. "Then we'll leave without you."

He steps up into the driver's seat and starts the engine.

ESCAPE

"Tash, get the yaks inside." Sam sprints to the front of the truck. He stands in the middle of the road, placing his hands on the hood.

The engine revs.

"Be careful!" I shout.

I try to think straight. A yak is used to the grasslands; miles and miles of open space. Being forced into a truck must feel like being trapped.

If they can't see maybe they won't be as scared.

I rip the bottom of my skirt. The woman rushes to help me. She holds Eve's nose while I fasten the fabric around her head.

"You're safe, Eve," I whisper into her furry ear. I lead her in a circle before I step up the ramp.

She sniffs the air with her large nostrils.

I nudge her forward and she takes another step. The fabric swings against her head and I tie the ends together, out of the way.

The truck's engine shuts off.

"Get out of the way!" shouts Jinpa.

I can't make out what Sam says. I dash over to Bones and lead him inside.

A door slams.

Jinpa marches around the right side of the truck holding Sam by his collar.

"You're not coming with us now," says Jinpa.

"They're only looking out for their animals," says the woman.

"She's right," says the younger man. "And the yaks are in now. Let's get out of here."

Jinpa reluctantly frees Sam and he sprints up the ramp to stand next to me. The men stride to the front of the truck and the woman approaches us.

"I'm Ness," she says calmly as she helps fasten the yaks' harnesses around metal handles welded to the sides. I sit down in a dusty corner, surrounded by dead flies.

"How long is the drive?" I ask.

"Twelve hours," Ness replies as she reaches out for one of the truck doors.

"What do we say if we get discovered?" asks Sam.

Jinpa leans into the remaining opening.

"There'll be nothing to say at that point. If I bang from the front you must hide immediately."

He slams the metal door and it shakes the whole truck. The squeaky latch is pulled across. We're locked in.

"Don't mind them," says Ness. "The events the other day have shaken them, that's all."

The engine rumbles and the rickety truck starts. It jolts over bumps and I'm thrown into the air for a split second. The yaks stamp. I have no idea where we're going but at least we're moving.

PHOTOGRAPH

Sam shines his flashlight around the truck. It's as colorful as a temple. He touches the masks. They're huge, painted with faces of snow lions, gods, and demons: the characters from Mom's stories.

"Did you make them?" I ask, reaching out and feeling the ridges of paint strokes beneath my fingers.

Ness nods. "I was a painter in a monastery."

"You're not wearing robes," says Sam.

"I know," she laughs. "I left."

"Why?" I ask, talking loudly over the rattling engine.

"It's not the same monastery anymore. It has changed since all the new laws."

I slip my hand into my pocket and pull out my Dalai Lama photograph. Ness looks straight at me and her eyes are kind but tired. It's the same way Mani looked and I wonder how I missed all this sadness before.

The motion of the wheels on the road turns smooth, but with a bump every second.

"We're going over a bridge," she says.

The bridge ends and the terrain is rockier than before. The fabrics sway above us.

"My friends made the journey," says Ness. "My sisters from the monastery."

"To India?" asks Sam.

She nods. "I know the way. I memorized the map in case I wanted to join them."

"Have you heard from them?" I ask.

"There's no way of getting information over the border but I think they made it safely. I can feel it," she says.

Several hours later, we stop to eat. The door creaks open and I climb out, next to a river.

We take turns leading the yaks back and forth to exercise on a grassy bank.

"Have you had any more ideas about the code?" I whisper to Sam.

He shakes his head.

"Come and eat," says the younger man, ushering us back to the truck. I shove the letter into my pocket. We gather inside, looking out through the open back door. The river, the mountains, and the sky are all a different shade of blue.

Jinpa is hunched next to a small gas burner, cooking. He passes me a bowl of warm thukpa. I slurp up the thick soup and noodles.

"Most of Asia's rivers come from up here," he says, gazing at the raging water below us. "The Dza Chu, the Dri Chu, and the Ma Chu."

I nod; I know that the rivers begin as glaciers before flowing into India, Thailand, or China.

"We need to drop them at the base of the path to India, next to the river," says Ness.

"Well, that's easier than trying to sneak them and two huge yaks into Lhasa." Jinpa smiles.

I sidle closer to the burner for warmth and watch the flame roar. I smell the gas and feel the heat. The vision around the corners of my eyes dissolves. I see a man within the center of the fire and watch the flames billow around him.

CHECKPOINT

Back on the road, the gears shift and the truck struggles uphill.

"We should try and sleep," says Sam. "While we can."

I close my eyes but they're jerked open again as we slam around a corner. I'm full after eating and hold my stomach. It groans as the soup swishes around inside.

The truck brakes. I brace myself for a sharp corner but the truck keeps getting slower and slower until it's crawling forward.

I strain to listen. There are three quick bangs against the metal at the front.

Sam's eyes snap open. He scrambles up.

"Hide," Ness whispers urgently. "Remember what Jinpa said."

I press the cold metal walls with my fingers, pushing at the floor. It's solid. There's no way we're getting out of here.

"Put these on," Ness says, throwing costumes at us.

I step inside the heavy material. It's too big and drapes over me. Grabbing a supply sack, I rip open the stitching with a stone and empty the food onto the floor. I throw it to Sam.

The truck stops moving.

"Get in," I say.

He shimmies into it and I stuff bundles on top of him until he's covered. The truck shudders as the engine is turned off. I pull a mask over my face.

Outside, I hear muffled voices. The back door rattles.

I hug my backpack and wriggle as far into the corner as I can. Ness covers me with piles of material. A musty smell floats around me.

The squeaky lock is unfastened.

The truck creaks under the weight of the yaks being led out. Boots thump up the metal ramp. A foot slams into my side. I'm knocked against the metal wall. It takes all my energy not to cry out.

This is it. My dragon luck has run out.

"Don't you worry," says a soldier. "If there's something here, we'll find it."

I hear another thud. He's moved on to Sam's sack.

Have they found him?

The thuds get quicker and more frequent.

Questions race through my mind. I'm as still as I can be and fighting the urge to cough. Dust coats the back of my throat, choking me.

"Anything?" asks a voice I haven't heard before. It booms outside the truck.

"Just costumes and food," says the soldier from before. "But I can tell he's hiding something."

"I pulled over another truck. I need you to search it."

"Just a few more minutes in here."

"I need you to search it now. Those are your orders." His tone is authoritative.

I hear hooves clomp up the ramp and then a thundering noise as the yaks gallop forward.

I squeeze my eyes shut.

The door squeaks.

I wait for Ness to say something to us; a whisper, a sign.

Nothing.

23

MAP

The engine splutters but I don't dare move.

What if there's still a soldier in the back?

I'm jolted about. My legs ache, and pins and needles shoot through my right foot. The air around me feels smaller and smaller.

Finally the truck slows to a stop.

"Safe!" yells Jinpa, unbolting the back. "It's safe."

I burst my head through the costumes, ripping the mask off my face. I smile at the yaks. Eve grunts when she sees me.

Where's Sam?

I crawl across the floor, digging through the

mess. I snatch at the sacks. He's buried under-neath, curled up in a ball. I shake him.

"Tash," he says, rolling over, "I'm fine."

I help him up and he stretches his legs.

Jinpa opens the door and I collapse into the sunlight, stiff and thirsty.

He passes me a bottle of water and I gulp it down. I pour some into my cupped hand and Eve's thick tongue slurps it up.

A row of mountain peaks stand in front of me. They're gray and rocky and snow-covered at the top.

The air is thin and I feel dizzy.

Ness draws her map from her pocket and holds it up for us.

There are three peaks: two small ones the same size and then a big one.

We crowd around her.

"You're heading between those two," Ness says, pointing at the dip next to the biggest one.

I nod.

"You'll see them when you head up from the river," she continues. "From then on, you go west. Make sure the North Star is on your right."

Mom used to teach me about the stars, but I don't remember where the North Star is now. I was always more interested in the stories that went along with them than actually locating them in the sky. I never thought I'd need to. I try to concentrate on the directions, but I can't help feeling we're in the middle of nowhere, miles and miles from home.

"Where's the river?" asks Sam.

"Go over that hill and you'll hit it. Continue upstream until you reach the tree that was split by lightning, then cut straight up into the mountains."

Sam repeats everything Ness says under his breath.

"Keep away from paths. The army patrols this area," warns Jinpa. "You can't be seen by anyone. It's the only route up to the mountains and the army will be on the lookout for people trying to escape over the border. They even pay the nomads to be informers."

I shiver. It's up to us now. And even when we do get home, it will be different. A man set himself on fire and nothing will be the same again.

RIVER

Jinpa slips a bundle of notes into my palm. Our money.

"We don't need it," he says. "And it's good to meet some young warriors."

"Thank you," I say simply.

Ness runs from the back of the truck, clutching a bag. "You'll need this," she says.

I peer inside. It's full of precious jerky and barley. Nestled between it all are the silver prongs of the gas burner.

"Take it," she says, climbing back in before we can refuse.

Jinpa pulls off, sticking his hand out the window and waving.

The truck disappears. We're alone in the mountains with one way out.

Sam loads the bags onto the yaks. I take Eve's harness and follow him up the bare rock filled with craters. It's what I imagine the moon to look like.

As soon as we're away from the road, we stop and look at the code again.

"It has to have something to do with the pictures of a quarter-moon," I say, pointing at it. "Otherwise why would they be there?"

"Yes, I think you're right!"

I grin at Sam. "I bet this is what it would be like if we were in the secret resistance together."

Sam looks thoughtful. "Maybe."

We hear the river before we see it, a steady roaring torrent. It cascades downhill, forming pools at each level. I rush toward it, scoop the icy water into my hands, and splash my face.

"Look out!" says Sam, jumping past me in his underwear and landing in the water with a splash.

Droplets hit me and I take off my clothes and slide in, washing away the dust and mess. The yaks lap the river water as we dry off in the strong sun.

We move more quickly after that, through the rock gorge carved by the frothy river. The yaks carry our supplies and we walk next to them. Birds dip and dive in the water.

"I need a break," says Sam, resting on a boulder.

"Dad says it's easier to get your breath back if you take a break by standing still," I say, stopping too.

Sam smiles. "Well, I'm not going to argue with your dad, but my legs could do with a rest."

I perch next to him. A line of ants crosses the boulder. I'm careful not to squash any as I sit down. I know every life is precious.

STARS

Night falls and I lie on the bumpy ground with the twinkling stars in the distance. The temperature has plummeted and I wrap my sleeping bag around me. There's a half-moon. I squint and its craters merge into the shape of a hare.

"Which one is the North Star?" asks Sam.

"I thought you knew," I reply, staring up at the millions of stars blending in and out of the Milky Way.

"So did I," says Sam. "But now I'm not so sure."

"Is it that bright one over there?" I ask.

"No, it can't be. There are too many stars around it."

Squeezing my eyes shut, I try to recall the story Mom told me.

Seven sisters were having a race. Two were tied in first place and two tied in second place. The fifth was close behind.

I stretch my sweater sleeve over my freezing fingers.

The sixth sister had to stop at the bathroom, and was farthest away. The seventh sister stayed at home and even now she never moves in the sky. That's the North Star.

I picture Mom's hand closed around a pen, tracing the constellation. I open my eyes.

"There it is." I spot it immediately. It seems obvious now. The stars are close; I could almost reach out and touch them.

I roll over to face Sam. His eyes are fixed on the sky.

"How did people navigate when it was cloudy?" he asks.

"Wait for a clear night, I suppose."

A wolf howls. I curl up close to Eve. I focus on my beating heart. I know Mom and Dad are still alive. My heart would feel different if they weren't.

✦ ✦ ✦

Sam shakes my arm and I wake, stiff and achy.

"Tash, look," he says. "We're right by it."

I force my eyes open. It's dawn and the sky has

an early-morning glow. The yaks lie next to me, misty breath streaming out of their nostrils. I must have slept for a few hours.

I turn my head to the side. On the slope is a tree, dead, black, and scorched. It's been split in two by a lightning strike. Two ravens perch on the top of it, cleaning each other's feathers.

Seeing it gives me a burst of energy.

"Let's go." I jump up and dust my clothes off; then I grab the water bottles and fill them in the river.

Sam leads the yaks to graze on the small patches of grass next to the riverbed and we fasten our supplies to them.

I scramble up the steep hill until my lungs feel like they're about to burst and I'm forced to zigzag back and forth, getting slowly higher. The yaks plod forward.

I don't take my eyes off the ground. One slip and I would crash down from the edge of the precipice.

"Do you think about the Man on Fire?" I ask Sam quietly.

"All the time," he replies.

I wait to see if he says anything else; I have so many questions.

"What if someone else tries to set themselves on fire?"

"There's nothing we can do," says Sam. "We just have to pray for their safety, like your parents said."

I turn and watch him closely. "How do you know that?" I ask. "You weren't with me when Mom said that."

"It must have been your dad," Sam answers quickly. "While you were making tea."

I narrow my eyes at him and he looks away.

MIGRATION

We climb higher and higher until I can no longer hear the river.

I've always loved being outside. Even in school I'd spend hours staring out the window, feeling like a prisoner and longing to be on the other side of the glass.

I look up. Mountain peaks, giant and rocky and snow-covered, stretch across the horizon in front of us: our white-tipped barrier. I open the map, holding it in front of me to compare it. Within the mountain range I see two small peaks followed by a big one.

"We're going the right way," I say, relief flooding over me. "From here on we follow the sunset."

My stomach groans and I rummage in the bag for a piece of jerky. I tear off a bite, getting the strings stuck in my teeth.

"I'm not so sure about this," murmurs Sam, staring up at the peaks. "It's too dangerous alone. We need help."

"Remember how you've always said that we can do anything?" I wave the secret eagle signal at him.

He signs it back.

"We were made for the mountains," I say. "Besides, we're not alone. We have the yaks."

Bones grunts and Sam smiles.

Eve stumbles on a loose rock and her body lurches forward. She snorts, picking her leg up and returning to her lumbering stride.

"You can do it too," I whisper.

We're surrounded by a rocky desert. Everything is still except for the shadows of clouds moving across the ground. Eve bends her head and munches on a shrub growing out of a crack. The branches stick out the side of her jaw.

"Look," says Sam. "The yaks need a break and I want to examine that letter again."

"Fine." I give in. I'm higher than I've ever been before and for the first time I can feel the lack of oxygen.

I unfold the letter.

"There are quarter-moons," says Sam. "There are four quarters in a whole, so let's try every fourth word."

We count.

"'How if more passing will mountains on and last is see or earliest,'" says Sam as he reads.

"That definitely doesn't make any sense."

"What about every fourth letter?" he asks.

It makes even more of a jumble. I sigh; we'll keep thinking.

Sam leads Bones to the bush. He rummages in the packs and pulls out the jerky. He rips a piece off and hands the rest to me.

"I was hungrier than I realized," I say, tearing the salty meat with my teeth.

"We're on rations," says Sam. "We're always going to be hungry."

I laugh, the icy air filling my lungs.

There's a sudden noise. I lift my head and scan our surroundings for somewhere to hide. There's nowhere that will disguise two yaks. Sam taps my arm and points. Two objects are in the sky, side by side and heading toward us.

For a second I think it's some kind of military airplane but then I hear the beating of air and the great flap of wings.

"Cranes!" says Sam.

I duck. They skim over our heads and head straight for the mountains.

They stop flapping when they reach the Himalayas, and soar. The wind catches the underside of their feathers. I hold my breath as they float upward, gliding on the current.

"I wish we could do that." Sam grins.

I nod. I'd give anything to be able to fly right now.

More birds appear, filling the sky with their waving wings.

The first pair is right at the top of the mountains. They cross over and disappear down the other side.

Then it hits me.

If the birds are migrating it means their lakes have already frozen.

Winter has arrived. The way will soon be blocked by snow.

We're running out of time.

WILDERNESS

I think about the moments we stopped along the way, all that wasted time.

"What if we get to the pass and can't get over it?" I say, unable to shake the image of a precipice from my mind.

Sam takes my hands in his. "We can do it." His voice is steady. "Remember what you were just saying. I wouldn't lie to you. I know you can make it."

Nerves stir in the pit of my stomach. The snowline creeps up, a vast whiteness that stretches endlessly in front of us. The snowdrifts fill the landscape with strange shapes. My boots make the snow crunch. Each time I pull my foot out, the slush gathers on my toes, and an icy cold wetness steadily sinks through to my skin.

The yaks have stopped. Eve scrapes at the snow with her front hooves, too cold to stand still.

Nothing prepared me for this, the never-ending cold and the aching that goes with it.

"We have to make a fire tonight," I say, grabbing Eve's harness and stroking her nose. "Or at least use the gas burner to cook something hot."

"What's on tonight's menu?" Sam asks jokingly.

"Momos with chili sauce, thenthuk, and soft fluffy tingmo bread," I reply. My mouth waters.

"Tsampa pancakes," says Sam.

"And yak cheese," I add. "Lots and lots of cheese."

"Enough!" says Sam, laughing and rubbing his sides. "My stomach can't take it."

We guide the yaks through the whiteness. Light reflects off everything. It stings my eyes, so I shade them with my hand. Tears stream down my face. The sun over the mountains casts angular shadows in every shade of gray.

"I can't see where we're going," I say.

"It's too bright," Sam agrees.

I glance at the yaks. At least Eve's big lashes

and shaggy long bangs protect her eyes from the merciless sun.

"Hang on," I say, rummaging in the bag for a knife. I kneel next to Eve and carefully cut a handful of hair from her long skirt, under her belly. It's not even enough to notice the difference.

"Here." I hand half to Sam. "This should help."

I wrap the hair around my eyes to prevent snow blindness. Fastening it at the back of my head, I can still see through the strands.

He grins. "We look like superheroes."

We walk single file. My thoughts drift. The man is on fire, running down the street, flames blazing behind him. My skin prickles. The wall of noise floods back. Dogs bark. The crowd shouts and cries and shuffles. I press my palms against my ears to block it out. The Man on Fire screams as he runs. "Freedom for Tibet!"

I replay everything that follows: the door crashing open, Mom's red skirt, Spaniel's sunken and shadowy eyes as he holds down Dad. But this time, I don't let the thoughts drown me. Instead, I take my fury and sadness and mull it over.

I won't let you down, Mom and Dad.

HIDE

We turn a corner, away from the big peaks. I look around and spot something that sends my hope crumbling to the ground.

Lined along the top of the mountain ridge, spaced at equal distances apart, is a row of snipers.

Sam follows my line of sight. His body stiffens next to me. His breathing turns shallow.

The snipers' guns point straight down the valley. I count five of them, watching and waiting for anyone who tries to cross the border. They'll pick us off one by one.

A lammergeyer soars on the mountain updraft, carrying a bone in its talons. It lets the bone drop and it plummets to the bottom of the valley, smashing on the rocks and echoing off the summits.

The snipers follow the sound with their guns; they can't have seen us yet. In that moment Dad's voice rushes back to me: *Always judge the situation.* I take a deep breath. If we don't disturb the stillness, we'll have a chance of escaping.

"Slowly," I whisper to Sam.

I fasten my hands around Eve's reins and nudge her backward. Bones is behind us. Every noise is amplified over the mountains.

Two steps back and we're out of sight.

Sam checks for more snipers.

"It's clear," he says.

The snow on the ground is scuffed where we retreated. On the ridge the snipers remain stationary, as if they've been frozen into the snow. The sniper closest to us adjusts his position.

"Go," I say to Sam.

I grab Eve's lead and plunge down the steep slope behind him. I slide across the snow. Thick mist masks the foot of the peak.

I sink into the snow up to my hip. The coldness hits my core. I push my hands down to pull myself out but they fall through the top layer, deep into the snow. I use my other leg as a lever. The snow closes around my thigh; I'm stuck.

Sam has almost reached the mist ahead of me. "Help!" I call.

He doesn't look back.

I thrash my arms in the snow. Flakes fly into the air. "Eve?" I call softly. "Come here."

She looks at me with her big brown eyes and hangs her head low with tiredness.

"That's it," I say, beckoning.

Eve lumbers forward and nudges me. I snatch her lead. She stands firm as I heave myself upward, out of the snow.

I wrap my arms around her neck and she grunts. Her body warms my shaking limbs. She lets me lean on her as we sprint down the slope. My teeth rattle from the cold.

"Tash!" Sam shouts, scrambling back up the slope. "What happened?"

"Fell," I say, too breathless to speak.

"I thought you were right behind me." He helps me onward, warming my hands in his. "I'm sorry. I'd never forgive myself if something happened to you."

As soon as we reach the mist, my legs collapse under me. I lie panting in the snow. Eve and Bones settle next to me while Sam stands guard.

"Why did no one warn us there would be snipers?" asks Sam.

"Like who?" I ask. "We don't know anyone who has done this before." I picture the ridge. "I think if we continue straight, we can climb up the mountain opposite and go around them."

The mist thickens and swirls around us. I listen for the sounds of soldiers. I imagine them stumbling across our tracks and following our footprints, guns raised.

All we can do is sit and wait for night to hide us.

LEAFLET

wake to find the mist has lifted and stars dot the cloudy dark sky.

My eyes adjust to the night quickly. I know the snipers are above us on the ridge. Their presence makes me shiver.

"This way," whispers Sam, pointing toward an overhang of snow. "We'll be more sheltered under there."

I stare at the ground. The muscles in my body are yelling at me to stop.

The clouds thin and the moon casts dappled light behind them. I hold my breath. The wind whooshes and carries the clouds across the sky.

"Come here, Bones," I whisper. "Eve."

They don't move.

If the snipers looked straight down they'd see Eve's tail sticking out from the overhang. I press my cheek against her soft neck, wrap my arm around her head, and coax her onward. Bones lumbers after us.

How many people have made it through the sniper valley?

I picture Sam's dad waiting for Sam to come home.

"Why didn't you tell your dad we were leaving?" I ask.

He shrugs. "He wouldn't have cared."

We walk all night, hiding from the moon, until the sun rises and I can see we've traveled way past the ridge with the snipers. At least, I think we have. Everything looks the same in the snow.

"Here?" asks Sam.

I nod, too exhausted to speak. We collapse on the ground. Sam passes me jerky. I chew and swallow before curling up in a ball next to Eve.

My mind spins with ideas about the secret message and I can't sleep. After a while, I open my backpack and pull out the copy of *The Snow Lion*. Perhaps there will be a clue in there.

For every lie Dad prints in his job, he tells a truth in the leaflet. I read the column under the **NEWS** section.

The Chodens are the eighth family to be taken in for questioning since the beginning of August.

I didn't realize it was so many people.

Their crimes include conspiracy against the Chinese government by performing songs in the Tibetan language. They haven't been seen since.

The importance of what Dad does hits me. If he didn't write this then no one would know about it.

The Chinese minister has scheduled a visit to the area, which will take place shortly.

I remember Dad mentioning it excitedly a while back.

I flick through *The Snow Lion*, looking for another clue, stopping under the section **TEACHINGS**. Mom always used to read that part to me. "The main purpose of the secret resistance is to preserve our culture," she'd say. "If we don't teach it then it will soon be forgotten."

I smile at the memory, but there's nothing in the leaflet that brings me any closer to figuring out the secret message.

TRACKS

Next day I wake early and spot tracks in the snow. Bending down to take a look, I trace them with my fingers. They're small, probably a fox. They remind me we're not alone in this emptiness, and something pulls me in their direction.

"Let's go that way," I say.

Sam lifts his head sleepily. "Why?"

"We should follow the fox."

He sighs. "Okay. But we need to be careful."

"We know there are snipers over there," I say, pointing behind us. "So let's keep going."

I lead us onward, placing my footsteps on

either side of the paw prints and trying to shake the doubt away.

"Dad will have to ask us to join the secret resistance when we get him back," I say.

"I don't know; we still have so much to learn."

"You sound like Dad," I say jokingly.

He shrugs.

I turn to him. "You remember when we were younger and I first found out about the resistance?"

Sam nods.

"And remember how desperate I was to join? Well, back then I only really cared because it was something I wasn't allowed to be part of."

My heart races. I've never admitted that to anyone before. Maybe I didn't even realize it until now.

Sam's staring at me, eyes narrowed.

"But now I really do want to help," I continue. "I'm ready, Sam."

"Then you should just tell your dad," he replies.

We keep walking, getting into our stride, until we turn a corner onto a thin path where another track crosses the fox's. I bend down and spread my fingers next to one. It's twice the size of my hand. At the top of it are lines, made by claws.

"Sam," I whisper. "A bear has been here."

He stares at the ground, following the trail with his eyes. The tracks appear from the drop to our right, cross our path, and disappear up the slope to our left.

The wind blows, carrying our scent straight toward the bear's path. I can't take my eyes off the ridge.

"We have to make noise," says Sam. "It's the only thing that will keep the bear away from us."

I glance at the folds in the mountain, imagining snipers hiding behind each one.

"There won't be more," says Sam, sensing my concern. "Not so close to the others."

I search the mountains again. There's no evidence of snipers, and the bear is what's worrying me most.

I open my mouth and sing. My quavering voice echoes off the snow and the mountain walls. No words come to my mind and I sing in vowel sounds to the tune Mom often hums.

"Let's go," says Sam, ushering me forward. "Hand me the prayer bowl."

I pass it to him and he clangs the wooden end of the mallet against it.

Eve shakes her head, startled by the noise.

Sam sings with me and we push onward, letting our voices clear the way.

I drag my feet around the next ridge. Sam pants beside me, singing between breaths. The bear tracks are far behind us now. My voice is raspy but I keep singing.

When we come up over the other side, I see the peaks again. Two big ones and a small one. It's just like the map.

We're going in the right direction.

The sun's setting behind them. The snow glows purple and we're bathed in pink light. It's the most beautiful sunset yet.

"Yes!" I punch the air.

Sam is beaming too. Eve moves next to me and nuzzles the palm of my hand. I rub her forehead, between the eyes. The yaks lie down and we climb up onto their backs and sit, side by side, watching the light change color as it gets dark.

MOON

When Sam stops and drops his backpack miles later, I don't complain. The snow is thinner and he shovels it aside with his foot. I lay the empty sacks on the ground and sit down on them to squeeze my shoes off. My feet are covered in blisters and my big toenail has peeled off. Yellow pus oozes in the corners.

I put my shoes back on and we take the tarpaulin and fasten it over the rock, making shelter from the battling wind. I pull the gas stove out, light a match, and turn it on. It whooshes up in a flame. I hold my hands over it. The flame withers and dies.

"No," I murmur. "Not now."

Sam finds two stones and places some dried dung between them. He sits in the entrance, striking match after match.

"Light," I say as the flame fades. "Please light."

A corner of the dung bursts into a small flicker of fire. Sam lets the flames grow, sheltering them with his hands and blowing to make them stronger. The smoke rises, dissolving into the sky. Sam balances the pot on top of the rocks and we scoop snow into it.

I hold my hands over the pot, loving the warmth. We pour in tsampa grain and it thickens into porridge.

"Brown sludge it is," says Sam.

I let the warm food slide down the back of my throat.

Watching the flames crackle, I blow on my spoonful and try not to gulp the porridge down in one bite. I've never been this hungry before.

"I know what it's like, remember," says Sam, gazing into the fire. "To lose a parent."

It takes a second for me to process Sam's words. When I do, heat flushes my cheeks and I can't believe what he's saying.

"They haven't died!"

"That's not what I meant," he replies quickly. "I understand what it's like when the world flips without warning and steals everything that was safe and real." Sam winds and unwinds Bones's hair around his finger.

It's the first time I've heard him talk about his mom.

"I'm sorry, Sam," I say, stroking Eve's fur.

"Do you know what helps?" he asks.

I shake my head.

"It's something my mom used to say when Grandpa first moved to the city," says Sam. "'Don't say you miss someone, say you remember them instead.'"

I think of the sound of Mom humming, the way Dad's eyes lit up when he finished writing a leaflet, and the time they took me sledging through the snows. Sam's right; I'll always remember those things.

I hold out some cooked tsampa to Eve. She sniffs it with her big nostrils and turns her head away. I push my palm back under her nose. She shakes her head, long shaggy hair swaying back and forth.

"Please," I say.

She ignores me.

"I thought they ate grains," I say, rummaging through the supplies.

I try mixing a tiny bit in some water and holding it out to her, cupped in my hands.

Eve raises her head and sniffs the air. She licks the water off my hand with her rough tongue.

"I'm sure they'll eat when they're hungry," says Sam.

I boil more snow and pour it into our metal water bottles. I hug mine close, thankful for the heat.

When the fire burns down to embers, Sam and I huddle next to it. The yaks lie on either side of us. Without them, I think we would have frozen already.

I rest my head on Eve and stare at the moon; it's a perfect crescent, just like in the picture on the letter. Eve's hair tickles my ear.

"We've been walking for a week," I say to Sam.

"How do you know?"

"It was a half-moon when we left Ness. Now it's a quarter-moon. It takes seven days for the moon to change from one to the other."

Sam stares up at the sky. "A quarter-moon is a seven-day cycle," he repeats.

We scrabble for the letter and crouch around it, shining the flashlight on the ink. Eve lifts her head as if to tell us to go back to sleep.

We count seven words and land on **yaks**. After that, it's **will**.

Sam and I stare at each other, eyes wide.

"Good so far," he says.

The next one is **fly**. My stomach drops.

"That doesn't make any sense," I say.

"Hang on, let's see." Sam keeps counting the words out. "'**Yaks will fly on the** . . . 11 . . . **November** . . .'" He looks up at me. "That has to be it."

"*Yaks will fly*? Are you sure?"

"Can you think of anything your dad said about yaks flying?"

I rack my brains but nothing comes to mind. "Eleventh of November. That date's in a few weeks' time," I say.

"Then we have until then to solve it."

GLACIERS

Next morning, I run the secret message through my mind as we walk.

"Time for a water break," Sam says, scooping snow into the pot.

I survey the last mountain in front of us; it's just as Ness said. One more pass to cross.

The snow below us gives way to a glacier, winding all the way down the side of the peak. It's steepest at the top. The ice glitters in the sunlight, slippery and smooth. A few weeks ago nothing would have stopped me from taking a sack and sliding down it.

I glance at Sam. He's grinning at me and I know he's thinking the same thing.

"We can't waste any time," I say.

"Just once isn't going to hurt," he says. "Besides, we have to wait for the water to melt."

Looking at the pot packed to the brim with snow and the tiny flame under it, I realize Sam's right. It will take at least a few minutes to melt.

"Just the first bit," I say. "We can't waste energy getting back up."

"Of course," says Sam, tying the yaks' lead ropes together to stop them wandering too far.

I remove one of the spare sacks and step into it.

"Race you to the bottom," says Sam.

It's like the old days.

"Ready," says Sam, "steady . . ."

I don't wait for "go." I'm off, using my hands to propel me forward. Gravity grabs me and I slip and slide across the ice. It crackles underneath me. I tug my hat off and the air rushes past my ears. My matted hair flies behind me. The glacier plunges downward and my stomach jumps.

"Whoop!" yells Sam behind me.

All my worry leaves me for a second as I slide away from it all. I glide across the ice, descending over the shadows in the dips and lines. Going over a bump, I lift into the air.

"Woo-hoo!" I call. My voice echoes back at me

from the mountains. I crash back down and my bones hurt but I'm laughing.

"Dalai Lama!" I shout. There's no one to stop me.

I never want it to end but I know it has to and I drag my fingers across the ice to stop. Mom told me that glaciers are constantly flowing but it's too slow to see. The ice creaks underneath me as I come to a halt.

"Watch out!" I say.

Sam crashes into me.

"Hey," I laugh, pushing him off and pulling my hat back on.

"That," he says, slapping the ice, "was the best thing in ages."

The slap makes a low note. He taps his other hand on the ice and it makes a different tone.

"Like drums," I say.

He nods and taps a rhythm. I join in. Once with my left, then two quick beats with my right. My fingers are numb. I clench and unclench them in between beats. Sam closes his eyes, throws his head back, and sings the song of the snow lion.

"We are the people of the mountains.
The mountain air runs through our veins.
We can breathe where others can't.
Mountain warriors of peace."

His voice cuts the freezing air. I think of Mom and Dad and pray that our song reaches them somehow.

The verse ends and Sam opens his eyes.

"I think we can do this, you know," he says. "As long as we have each other."

"And the yaks," I say, looking up at Eve waiting patiently at the top. I squint. Another figure joins her.

Adrenaline shoots through my blood and the familiar feeling of danger comes booming back in an instant.

"Sam," I say, tapping his arm. "There's someone up there."

LEADER

I stop thinking. I just want Eve and Bones to be safe. My legs slip on the glacier.

Three figures watch us scramble up.

I claw at the ice, pulling myself up faster.

"It could be soldiers," says Sam. "And we're outnumbered." His heavy breaths are right behind me.

I don't slow down. All I know is I have to protect the yaks. I made a promise to Mani.

I'm shaking with frustration. I let myself get distracted, laughing and playing while the snipers snuck up on us.

I heave myself onto the ridge. We're surrounded by hooded figures but they're not
soldiers. They're nomads.

Where's the backpack?

I can't see it. I whip my head around and catch
the glint of the copper prayer bowl in the sun.

Our bags are on the ground, their contents
spilling onto the snow.

I remember Jinpa's warnings about nomads
being paid to be informers.

Sam catches up, leaning over to get his breath
back.

"Tash," he whispers in my ear. "Get away
from them."

I shake him off. They have my backpack. The
letter is in the front pocket. The *Snow Lion* leaflet
is in the main compartment.

"Wait," says a man. The way he carries himself is different, distinctive. He stands up tall
and straight.

He must be their leader.

"We've been expecting you," he says.

Sam and I look at each other.

"What do you mean?" asks Sam.

"Don't you have something for us?" He nar-
rows his eyes and turns a compass over and over
in his palm.

"No," says Sam.

The nomads shuffle back and forth, whispering together and gazing around us.

"Is it just you boys here?" the Leader asks.

I'm puzzled for a second; then I nod, remembering my disguise.

"Where did you get this backpack from?" asks the Leader.

"We found it on the route," says Sam quickly. "Thought it might be useful."

The Leader watches us closely, as if he's trying to determine whether we're telling the truth.

"Thank you," he says eventually. "You might not realize it but you delivered something very important."

I feel Sam looking at me. I know we're both thinking the same thing: *Is it the letter?*

"What do you mean?" I ask.

"It's dangerous out here. We could be watched. Let's get everyone back to camp." He nods toward his men and avoids the question. "Come and stay with us. Have a proper meal."

I hesitate, unsure whether he can be trusted. But one thing I do know is that I have to keep the backpack safe. If they are informers then it holds all the evidence they need.

The nomads lead us over a ridge and then steeply down between two cliff edges. It's dark, cold, and wet.

I map our movements in my mind. With every step down we go farther away from the Dalai Lama. We have to be able to get back here.

"You and your yaks look like you could do with some food. Been on the road for a while?"

"A few days."

I clench my teeth; I'm not going to give them too much information.

We emerge into a clearing. Two rectangular white tents stand side by side on flat ground next to a barren mountain. Beyond it, a herd of yaks graze in front of a lake shaped like a butterfly. It's mostly frozen but I see the reflection of the sky and the clouds in the watery parts.

Stepping on patches of pasture, I wonder how long it would take to know the mountains this well, to be able to find the glacial lakes and the grass within the rocky emptiness.

NOMADS

Eve and Bones are led off to join the herd and Sam and I are taken closer to one of the tents. It glows brightly, with the symbol of the endless knot painted on the side.

There's a fire in the middle and it's instantly warm when we step inside. Patterned rugs overlap each other on the floor. Cooking equipment hangs from hooks in the back corner. Our supply bags are added to a heap.

We sit cross-legged on the rugs. A man places steaming cups of butter tea and a piece of yak cheese in front of us. I slide Dad's heavy coat off and fold it behind me. I remove my hat and my hair tumbles down around my ears. I catch the Leader staring at me quizzically. Sam pokes my foot and I yank my hat back on.

Sam takes a sip of tea.

I sniff it and my stomach rumbles. I dip my tongue in. It tastes like home. The buttery salty broth warms my body and before I can stop myself, I gulp it down.

Throughout the day, the tent is a flurry of activity with the clanking of cooking pots and the boiling of broth. One man feeds the fire in the center of the tent. The comforting smell of stew makes my stomach turn with hunger and reminds me of my house.

Afternoon turns into evening and a nomad with a damaged foot limps over, carrying a tray with bowls of food on it. I'm puzzled; I didn't expect them to take such good care of us. It makes me want to trust them, to spill everything and ask for their help. But it's too risky.

There are five people in the tent now, settling down to sleep on sheepskin rugs. I curl up, pretending to be asleep and observing them through half-closed eyes.

When the only noise left in the tent is the slow snoring of the nomads, I nudge Sam and he pulls his penknife from his belt. In one swift movement he stabs the bottom of the tent. Dragging his hand across, he slits the seam. It tears loudly. One of the sleeping men coughs and rolls over.

Go, mouths Sam.

I nod and tiptoe toward the backpack. Seizing it, I check inside. The letter is gone.

I see papers on top of the one table in the tent and shuffle toward it.

The leaflet is there, wedged between the pages of a book.

"Yes," I whisper, tucking it into my pocket.

I spot our supply bags neatly stacked next to the table. We'll never survive without them.

I seize the string around our bags and lift them as quietly as I can. I bump into a leg and stumble. The nomad shifts position. His eyes are shut. I stay as still as a Buddha statue.

Sam holds up the side of the tent. It creates a draft of icy air. He beckons at me to follow him.

I haven't got the letter, I mouth at him.

"Leave it," he hisses. "They won't know what it is."

My forearms burn with the weight and I tremble as I creep back to Sam.

Sam dashes forward, grabs the bags, and ushers me in front of him. I duck and roll underneath the cover. The air is cold and I can see my breath. I wait for my eyes to adjust to the darkness.

"Quick," says Sam.

I pull myself away from the tent, toward the yaks, who are casting long shadows in front of me.

We creep forward on our hands and knees, dragging the bags behind us. My skin grazes the stones. I scan the yak field. There's a look-out guard sitting on the other side. His head is tipped in a heavy way that tells me he's asleep. I tug Sam's leg and we stand slowly, not making a sound.

The yaks are free in the herd. I spot Eve immediately; she's the smallest of them. I run toward her. My feet rustle the grass. Bones is close by; the white stripe across his eyes is lit up by the moon.

"Eve," I whisper. "It's me."

She munches on the piles of cut grass. A small untouched bundle lies next to her.

"Get that grass," I whisper to Sam.

Several of the resting yaks heave themselves up, swishing their horns from side to side.

"Let's go, Eve," I say.

PURSUIT

Eve pads across the grassy carpet and Bones tags after her. We hurry onward. We soon reach the snow, where the landscape is flooded by an eerie grayness. It's only then I sneak a look behind us. There's a light moving in the distance.

"Someone's following us," I say.

Sam glances at the light. "We have to stay ahead." He smiles.

"Why are you grinning?" I ask.

He uncurls his hand. A circular object drops and swings from his fingertips. It's a compass.

"How did you get that?" I ask.

"The Leader dropped it near us. I hid it with my feet. He didn't notice."

"Sam," I say, hugging him. "You star!"

I clasp it in my hands, spinning the compass around until the arrow matches north. We're headed west, going in the right direction.

"Do you think they were informers?" I ask.

"Yes," he says. "They're as bad as the snipers." He grimaces, jutting his chin out, and steps forward with his jaw clenched and a new determination in his stride. We stare at each other. I've seen that look before. It's the same expression the Man on Fire had.

I fight to not let my mind be back there again, among the flames and the screaming people. I focus on my boots; I've learned that looking at one detail of my surroundings can help keep me grounded.

My mind wanders to the code.

Yaks will fly. Yaks will fly. Yaks will fly.

"Why couldn't Dad just have told me what was going on?" I say, frustration prickling down the back of my neck.

"He was trying to protect you, to keep you safe," Sam answers softly.

With the compass we move more quickly. I take the lead, staring down at the arrow.

Sam shakes his head. "This is harder than I

expected. Thousands of people have made this crossing. They even said the Dalai Lama did it when he fled Tibet. It sounded easy."

"No one can call this easy," I say.

I look at the dark shadow of the mountain, its sheer granite walls and endless stretches of ice glaciers. I pray that we've gotten all the bad luck over with.

We walk alongside the precipice, a deep slit in the earth. As we get farther away, lost in the mountains, it becomes hard to imagine the way home.

"I never want to walk this much again," says Sam.

"Once we've rested it will be easier," I reply, thinking about the journey back. "Maybe the Dalai Lama will send us home in our own plane."

I rehearse how I'll tell him about the soldiers and my parents being taken.

"I'm not sure the Dalai Lama can do things like that," says Sam.

I shrug. "Dad will sort it all out."

Sam grows silent. "Do you ever worry that we won't be able to go back?"

I think of Mani and Sam's dad, of Dorjee, his sister, and everyone else at home. "If we can make it to India," I say, "then somehow we'll be able to get back."

Sam strokes Bones's nose.

Spotting a crossing over the precipice, I run and kneel by it. A small, rickety rope bridge hangs across the six-foot crack in the ground.

"Will it hold the weight of the yaks?" I ask.

Sam crouches and presses down on the first wooden slat. It swings and creaks. Underneath is the deepest darkness. Sam crawls onto it. I hold my breath, only able to wait and watch. The first slat cracks but doesn't break and Sam inches onward.

Finally, he reaches the snow on the other side. "That slat is thin," he says, standing. "The rest are strong enough."

Sam calls Bones and gently tugs him across. The wood groans underneath them. Once they're over, Sam spins around, beckoning.

It's my turn.

I tread on the plank and feel it swing.

"Quick, Eve," I say, leading her behind me.

I'm sure the bridge could collapse at any second.

I sink to my hands and knees and grasp the wooden edges. My skin is dry and my knuckles are cracked.

I edge forward without looking down. Pressing on the last slat with my knees, I hear it split. I dive to the ground.

Sam darts toward Eve. I turn to see the slat dangling down in two halves. Eve straddles the broken pieces: front hooves on the ground, back hooves resting on the slat before. She lifts her back leg into the air, searching for solid ground. Her hoof touches the snow, then slips. I jump up and clutch her head and horns.

"Pull," says Sam, reaching for her harness.

I dig my foot into the snow for purchase and try to shift Eve's weight toward us.

She grunts, bends her front legs, and heaves herself off the bridge, stumbling onto the snow.

"You're safe," I say, stroking her neck and feeling her heartbeat race.

I've learned to read Eve like she's my sister. Every grunt tells me whether she's tired or hungry or wants attention. I curl up to her every night. My lips are too raw to whistle but if I tilt my head she knows to follow.

I spread the grass we took from the nomads in front of the yaks and they finish it in one go. We let Eve calm down before nudging her onward. I picture what we look like from a distance—boy, yak, girl, yak; four tiny figures crossing the vertical sheer rock mountain, all striving to blend into the wilderness—because no matter how hard I try, I can't shake the feeling that we're being followed.

THUNDER

That evening Eve starts limping. I pull her leg up and examine her hoof, as I've seen Mani do. I can't see any signs of damage.

I'm becoming an expert at pushing thoughts out of my head. But every now and then, the image of a man surrounded by flames comes rushing back.

"Why do you think he did it?" I ask Sam. "The Man on Fire, I mean."

"If you protest peacefully the soldiers take you away," he says, folding his arms across his chest. "It's the same thing in the end. Except that more people will pay attention. It's harder to hide that kind of protest from the outside."

I stare at him.

"I'm sure there are other ways," I say. "There have to be."

"You don't understand." Sam has a glazed look on his face. "He wanted to protect us. It was a form of protest. He thought if people realized how bad it was, then they would do something about it."

"But he hasn't protected us," I say. "He was the reason Mom and Dad were taken. It's his fault."

"It wasn't, Tash. It was the soldiers and the rules and everything else. Don't blame him."

He's someone I don't recognize, full of a new anger that scares me. We've always understood each other before. I touch the photograph in my coat, wishing Mom and Dad were here. They'd know what to say.

Thunder rumbles over the mountains. Unless we find somewhere to camp soon, we'll be caught in a storm. I think about making a snow cave but it's too much effort. We'd never be able to fit the yaks in anyway.

Big raindrops of freezing water sting my ears and water drips inside my collar. I shiver, tightening my hood around my face. The clouds hang low in the sky, swallowing the moon and stars. There's a crack as lightning strikes. For a split second it illuminates the white snow around us.

"One elephant," I whisper. "Two elephants, three . . ."

Thunder booms. It shakes through my body.

"It's close!" I shout to Sam.

Sam passes me Bones's lead. He scrambles up a small ridge.

"What are you doing?" I shout. "You'll be hit by lightning!"

A bolt forks out of the sky, like a purple branch reaching out of the clouds.

"Sam!" I shout. "Get down!"

"I can see a cave," he yells, "just over there! It's not much farther."

Thunder claps above me. Bones pulls on the lead, stepping backward with wide eyes.

"This way," says Sam, taking Bones and beckoning me toward the ridge.

I walk but Eve refuses to move.

"Just a bit farther," I say, tugging at the lead.

She limps and nudges my hand with her cold, wet nose.

"Come on, Eve," I say, stroking her head. Icicles cling to the ends of her matted hair.

"Tash!" yells Sam, shining a flashlight on me. "Get in here!"

I wrap my arms around Eve's head, cover her eyes, and push her forward.

MANDALA

The roar of the thunder is muted. Sam shines the flashlight up the walls. The cave is just big enough for us all.

Eve shakes her coat, spraying water drops on us. Bones nervously lifts his hooves. Sam strokes him, soothing him.

I rub Eve's muzzle, feeling the soft bit above her nose, between her eyes.

Sam squats and builds a fire close to the entrance. It's wet and just a tiny flame ignites, but it calms Eve and she sinks to her knees and lies down. I cuddle up to her wet coat.

Sam picks up some charcoal from the fire and

draws a circle around us. It scrapes across the floor. He adds a zigzag pattern and forms an inner circle.

"A mandala," he says. I smile; it represents the universe and sacred space. When we're inside it, we're safe.

"What about the yaks?" I ask.

He gets back on his hands and knees and crawls around them, drawing another circle.

"There," he says. "Now we're all safe."

Eve licks it with her long leathery tongue.

"I'm sorry it's not food," I whisper. I try again to feed her grains but she won't eat anything.

I glance around the dark pebbly edges of the cave, half expecting to see a bear.

Pulling the copy of *The Snow Lion* from my pocket, I open it again.

Sam snatches the piece of paper out of my hand. "We've got more important things to worry about, like what on earth we do when we see the Dalai Lama."

"What are you doing?" I grab it back. It tears down the middle. I seize the other half from his fingers and hold both pieces close to my chest.

"My dad wrote those words," I say. "This is all I have of him right now." I glare at Sam, my breathing shallow and fast.

He looks into the fire.

The flames crackle in his pupils.

"Tash," he says. "I'm sorry. It's just . . . I need to tell you something. Something I should have already told you." His eyes are serious and sad. He's never looked at me like this before.

"What?" I ask. "What is it?"

"Just before we left, I joined the resistance with your parents."

His words form a wall that slams into me.

"You're lying," I say. But I know he's telling the truth. I just don't want to believe it. "Why didn't you tell me?"

"One of the rules is that we can't tell anyone. They say trust no one."

It takes a second for his words to register with me. We always promised to tell each other everything. I close my fists and think of our eagle signal. It's meaningless now. "You talk about the truth, and all the time you were lying to me, Sam. You were lying!"

"I know. I'm sorry."

"Are you?" I ask. "Or is that just another lie?"

The fire reaches a grassy bit of dung and sparks and fizzes, matching the anger I feel inside. "If you don't trust me then why are you coming with me?"

"It's not like that," says Sam. "I want to help you."

"I don't want help from a liar!" I yell. Pure hurt pours from my mouth.

I picture Mom, Dad, and Sam sharing secrets together, laughing behind my back.

"I know what you've been doing this whole time," I say. "You've been stealing my family because your dad doesn't care about you!"

There's a silence, and I can feel the pain surging out of him.

"You want me gone?" he asks, his cheeks flashing red.

He pauses, waiting for my response. I shrink inside myself.

"Fine. Come on, Bones." He disappears, swallowed by the blackness outside.

The shadows claw up the cave walls. I reach out and touch the cold sides to steady myself.

"Don't go," I whisper.

It's too late.

My voice echoes around the empty cave.

38

ALONE

I stay in the cave all night with Eve, trying to make sense of everything. I rest my head against her shaggy long hair. I think back over the past month: the times Sam worried about trouble with the soldiers, the hushed conversations he shared with Dad, even the way he knew the letter was a secret message.

Why wouldn't Mom and Dad want me to join the resistance? I could be as much help as anyone. I know it.

Eve grunts and I stroke her ears. She has kept watch with me all night. My clothes are damp from the storm and I shiver as the coldness seeps into my skin.

I close my eyes, trying to unscramble my thoughts.

I wonder just how many people are in the resistance and think about the different reasons they might have joined. I know I'm not the only one with parents in prison.

Sam should have returned by now. He must be heading back to our town.

He really has gone.

I stop and focus on the only thing I know to be true.

I need to get to the Dalai Lama.

The wind whistles, sending a chill up my spine. The rain's finally stopped and the storm is farther away. It's beginning to get light.

With Sam gone, I'm scared to leave the mandala circle.

I glance at the supplies. Time is ticking and I'm running low. There's probably only enough food for a day or two. Sam left with Bones and one of the supply bags; he has half of everything.

Slowing my breathing, I crawl to the edge and step outside the circle.

"Okay, Eve," I say. "It's me and you. We're almost there."

Outside the cave, there's an eerie wet mist that swamps everything. I can hardly see in front of me. I slip, grabbing onto Eve to stop myself from falling. She's thin. Her matted skirt of thick hair hides the rib cage I feel underneath.

"Why haven't you been eating?" I yell at her.

Instantly I hug her neck. "I'm sorry," I say, gripping her shaggy coat.

We battle onward, up the steep slope.

"This is the last mountain," I tell Eve. "After this we'll have made it."

It sleets. Icy arrows shoot from the sky and sting my face. My feet slip.

I look around for another cave. I'm drenched and icicles cling to Eve's hair.

We can't go on.

"Let's turn back," I say. "We'll rest and I'll find you some food." I'm shivering badly. I lead her around.

She trips.

All her weight thuds to the ground as she falls onto her side. Her head smashes into the snow and flakes flurry into the air.

"Eve!" I shout, dropping to my knees next to her.

I stroke her head. She looks up at me with tired eyes.

"Come on, Eve," I plead. "Get up."

She lifts her head, then rests it back down. Panic tightens in my chest.

"Help me!" I shout.

But there's no one there.

A blizzard roars and snow tumbles out of the sky. Pushing her shoulder up with my knees, I try to get her to budge.

"Get up, Eve!" I tug at her horns.

I sink into the snow next to her head. Our foreheads touch. Her nostrils flare with her fast panting breath. It warms my face.

"Please, Eve," I beg.

The snow piles up around us.

My body is numb. I know we can't stay here for long.

"We'll rest," I say. "Just for a minute."

I wish Sam was here.

Eve's breathing quickens. She grumbles on every exhalation.

I curl up into her, burying my head into her neck. I taste my salty tears before they freeze. The snow is the softest blanket. My muscles no longer ache. My body feels heavy. I'm already drifting into a dreamworld. I can see Mom, Dad, and Sam. Everything will be better if I just close my eyes.

SNOWS

I take a sharp breath. Oxygen shoots to my head. I'm upside down, wrapped in layers of blankets and slung over Sam's shoulder.

Sam.

Sharp stinging shoots up and down my body. Sam rests me on Bones. I hug his neck and let the yak's body warm mine.

"I shouldn't have left," Sam says quietly. "I'm sorry. I tried to find you sooner but I got lost." He takes my feet in his hands and rubs them.

There's no feeling in my soles. "It's too late," I say. I know what frostbite is, how the blood stops circulating to your toes and then they fall off.

Sam keeps on moving my feet. "When I got back to the cave you were gone. I do trust you. You have to believe me."

"Eve," I say, lifting my head and looking around. "Where's Eve?"

Sam is quiet. His long matted hair falls in front of his face.

I turn, expecting to see her sitting behind us, watching me from under her big eyelashes, but she's not there. Only one set of hoofprints winds down the mountain.

My heart rips in two.

Eve protected me. She saved my life.

"I'm so sorry, Tash."

His voice sounds far away. I think of Eve and it's too much to bear. I feel as if I'm falling and let myself slip into the darkness.

The next time I open my eyes, Sam's built a fire with the last of the dung. I'm wrapped up in everything we have with us. I move my arms and stretch my legs. The circulation slowly comes back. I point and flex my feet. I can feel them.

"How bad are they?" I ask.

"Tash," Sam says, jumping up and rushing toward me. "I think they'll be okay." He dashes over to the pot resting on two stones and pours steaming broth into a cup. He wraps my fingers around it. My body feels like it needs to sleep for a million years. I take a sip and the warmth of the soup spreads down my throat and into my belly.

How long have I been out?

It's light, but gloomy, as if the sun never rose properly.

I take a pained breath as I replay what happened. Eve can't be gone. I hug my knees to my chest. Mani needs her. I need her.

"Where is she?" I ask.

"You were lying in the snow together when I found you," Sam replies. "Up there." He gestures to the top of the slope.

"I have to see her."

Sam tilts his head toward me. "It's pretty far up."

"I have to check." I hear my voice quaver. "I have to be certain."

Sam nods and helps me stand. We link arms and together we limp through the land of snows to find Eve.

BURIAL

E ve lies peacefully in the snow. When I touch her coat it's cold, and I know that life has left her body. It's just flesh now. I kneel next to her and brush the thin layer of snow away. Grief grips me and squeezes my chest.

I let her down. This wasn't meant to happen.

I think back to Sam's mom's funeral and the walk up two hundred steps into the clouds, where we laid her body on rocks to be taken by sky dancers. We're even higher here.

"I want to give her a sky burial," I say.

"Are you sure?" asks Sam.

I nod. I can't help feeling that this is my fault.

I'm the one who insisted we bring the yaks. I'm the one who pushed her out into the snow. I have to say goodbye to her in the proper way. The traditional way. I owe her that.

Bones stands over Eve. He lowers his head and nudges her with his horns.

"She's not coming back, Bones," says Sam.

"Not in this body," I say.

I pretend the smoking dung is juniper incense and wave it over her body with my shaky hand. I say a prayer for her.

"Thank you, Eve, our loyal companion. Your life was precious."

Even though I hear the words, it doesn't feel real. I keep expecting Eve to grunt and lift her head. But she stays motionless.

I'm so sorry. I miss you.

I can't bring myself to say it out loud.

"Hand me your knife," I say to Sam.

I cut off some of her hair and hold clumps of it in my hand. Then I rip the lining of my coat open and stuff the mass inside. Her hair gives me an extra layer of warmth.

Sam is still next to me. I know he must be thinking about his mom. I reach out and touch his arm. When Sam's mom died, Dad taught me about rebirth and how, after death, you return to the world in a new body. Afterward, I looked for Sam's mom in every newborn child, animal, and insect.

"What do you think Eve will come back as?"

"She was already the best a yak could be," replies Sam. "So maybe she'll be a human."

I remember the way Eve looked after me, how she'd stop to check that I was still walking behind her and nuzzle my arms to keep me warm. She had the kindest of hearts.

"She'll be a wonderful person." I sink down into the snow next to her. "How will I ever tell Mani?" I ask quietly.

"Mani may be old but he can look after himself. You don't need to worry about him right now," says Sam gently. "You can't blame yourself."

Except I do. It's hard not to see her death as a sign that I'm doing the wrong thing. Without Mom and Dad here, how am I supposed to know what to do?

I look up to the mountain peaks, willing my parents to appear and tell me how to keep going.

We're quiet for a while, watching Eve together. The wind scatters snow across the ground in shapes and swirls. Sam squeezes my shoulder and I realize the answer is next to me.

"Sam, can you call them?" I ask.

"Are you sure?" he mumbles.

"It's time," I say. Tears stream down my face. The wind freezes them against my cheeks.

Sam throws his head back, his long hair dangling past his shoulders. He looks older as he opens his mouth into an oval. From the back of his throat he makes the rasping call of the vultures.

The sky is still.

"Try again," I say.

He calls, straining to be louder this time.

The noise echoes off the mountains. I stare up at the sky. There is one fluffy cloud in front of the peak.

"They're not here," says Sam.

Then, suddenly, I see them. The sky is full of big birds, circling and soaring. The black tips of their wings ruffle. They swoop down, stumbling and falling over as they land, beating their wings to steady themselves. They shuffle toward Eve, with their curved beaks and hunched shoulders.

"Let's go," I say, and I grip his hand in mine as the two of us turn to leave together.

PROTEST

We're silent for a long time after that. Instead of speaking, Sam keeps turning to stare at me with deep, searching looks that are far worse than any scolding. They stir up my stomach.

"Are your feet hurting?" he asks eventually. "We can take a rest."

"I'm fine," I say, shaking my head.

I'm longing to know more about what he's been hiding from me but it doesn't feel right to talk about it yet.

We push on, the final pass ahead of us, between two big peaks. The rock is packed in with snow and it levels where the two mountains meet. That's where we're heading. That's what we have to climb over.

I focus on the compass, grasping the cold metal in my hand. I make sure the arrow is lined up with north, and check that we're heading west. I stare at it as I walk. It takes my mind off Sam and Eve.

"Watch where you're going!" says Sam.

I've drifted close to the edge of the path. It shakes me. I'm tired and achy.

"Can I take it for a while?" asks Sam.

I nod. I feel like I'm sleepwalking.

He drops the compass into his breast pocket and pats it with his hand. "Don't worry," he says. "I won't let us get lost. We're almost there."

I walk next to Bones, plodding forward through the snow and holding his wiry hair for support.

Wispy clouds stretch across the sky, turning pink and orange under the setting sun. A shadow grows up the mountain as the sun gets lower.

"Listen," Sam says. "All your dad wanted me to do was make sure you were safe."

"That's what friends do," I say. "You don't have to be in the resistance for that."

He doesn't reply.

There's nowhere to rest and camp. A snow cock with dappled white feathers dashes across our path.

"Do you want to stop?" asks Sam.

I shake my head, driven forward by the thought of my parents. We walk on into the night until, finally, I step onto a flat ridge and collapse.

"Let's rest," I say.

We're too exhausted to make a fire; we break the last of our food up into piles. Our flashlight is dim.

I try to chew the jerky slowly but my stomach longs for it and my mouth takes over. I swallow the meat.

Sam watches me. I know he's wondering what I'm thinking.

"I wasn't joking earlier. You know the only reason your dad didn't ask you to join was because he didn't want to put you in danger. Well, I know how he feels."

"You think I can't protect myself?" I ask.

"No. I've seen you with the soldiers and the nomads. You can be tougher than anyone. But you are so loved, Tash."

I nod, thinking of Mom and Dad and how I have to see them again.

"You have to admit you can be a little reckless," Sam says jokingly.

"No I don't," I say. I'm defensive at first but
then I think of the running and the soldiers. I
wouldn't do those things now, not after everything I've learned. "I guess I was a little bit
reckless," I add.

Sam smiles. "Everything your parents do is
dangerous as well, but they're trying to help
people and make things better."

"Maybe it's time I found new ways to protest,"
I concede.

We grow silent for a while, lying next to each
other. He reaches out and touches my hand.

"I'm sorry," he says.

He should have known he can trust me. But I can see
from the look on his face that he's trying to make
everything right.

"I forgive you," I say. And I mean it. "Tell me
more about the Man on Fire."

"People are angry, Tash. They're desperate
for the situation to change but they can't resort
to violence. They can't go to war or fight."

"The Man on Fire, was he part of the
resistance?"

"No."

I wrap my blanket tighter around me.

"I didn't mean what I said," I say. "About you
stealing my family, or that your dad doesn't care
about you. He does."

"I know," says Sam.

Feeling closer to the stars than ever before, I spot one that's red and doesn't twinkle. I bet it's a planet. I wonder if Mom and Dad can see it from wherever they are.

ASCENT

At last we make the final ascent over the pass. Even though it's covered in snow, I can see the shape of the mountain underneath. We'll be able to navigate a path around the ice gullies and crevasses.

"It's not blocked," I say, relieved.

Sam smiles at me. "It's time we had some good luck."

The snow is compacted and slippery. I dig my heel in, making a foothold, before I step.

My lips are cracked and my hands dry and weathered. The wind whistles past us, picking up a layer of snow and blowing it across our path. It stings my ears and I yank my hat farther down.

"This is the highest we'll ever be," Sam says, out of breath and stepping onto the last ridge.

"The only time I ever want to do this again," I say, "is if it's on the way home."

A cloud passes and I can almost reach out and touch it.

The layers of mountains stretch out before me. I didn't realize how big the Himalayas are and just how many mountains rise out of the earth. The air is thin and I can hardly breathe. Pressure builds in my nose.

Bones grunts. He's already heading back down the other side of the slope. I know we should be close behind him. It's not good to stay up here for too long but I can't get my feet to go any faster.

At the pinnacle I take one last look around. I'm on top of the world. Sam and I smile at each other. Making it up here means we are able to achieve anything. Yet at the same time, the mountains leave me feeling as tiny as an ant.

We're so small. Can we really make a difference?

"Come on," says Sam, beckoning toward the way down.

"Just one more second," I say. In the distance I can see India; behind me, Tibet. I stare, transfixed. I don't want to take my eyes off it. I never want to forget it. The sky and the peaks melt into one.

We make it down the other side, through the thick snow. I focus on putting one foot in front of the other as Bones lollops forward beside me. I pray we find grass for him to eat soon. I remove the empty supply bags and unbuckle his harness. I leave almost everything behind, carrying nothing but *The Snow Lion* and the Dalai Lama photograph.

Suddenly I see it: a white stone monument rising out of the snow in the distance. Strings of yellow, green, red, white, and blue prayer flags crisscross it, tangled with each other. Some are faded and torn and newer brighter ones rest on top of them. After the endless white of the snow and the gray of the sky, it feels like I'm seeing color for the first time. I can't take my eyes off it.

The flags flutter in the breeze. I breathe deep into my belly, letting the cold air rush into my lungs. The wind lifts my hair and tickles my ears. It whispers the prayers from the flags to me. I stand, feet rooted in the snow, swaying gently, letting the feeling of happiness flood over me.

The monument marks the border.

India.

Butterflies gather in my stomach.

We've made it.

I picture the Dalai Lama. I've practiced my speech so many times in my head. Soon I'll get to say it aloud.

It's just as I imagined. All we have to do is follow the winding ridge path. I squint, trying to figure out how long it will take.

"Only an hour away," I guess.

"Or maybe a bit longer, in our present state," says Sam.

I bend down and scoop a snowball toward him. I'm weak and it lands just in front of me.

Sam doesn't even duck but he smiles.

I tuck my fingers back inside my sweater, under my armpit.

"We should go," says Sam, holding out his hand. His hair is frozen and stuck to the side of his face. "Think you can manage?"

"Of course," I say, but I take his hand to balance, clutching it tightly.

The snow in front of us is untouched except for the paw prints of a wolf. We hobble forward, hand in hand, tracking a new path. Every footstep makes my body ache, but inside I'm dancing.

SAM

"Just think," says Sam. "Soon we can have hot food."

"Yak cheese and butter tea," I say, "that's all I want right now."

The thought drives me forward.

We turn a corner.

A gunshot echoes off the mountains. Panic ripples up my spine. Ringing fills my ears. All other sound disappears. It's as if the gun has sucked everything in and fired it back out in a single note.

Sam dives to the ground, yanking me with him. My head knocks into the compacted snow.

It stings my face, pulling my skin tight. The snow slushes into my mouth.

Hooves thunder against the ground. Bones bolts, kicking snow up behind him.

Run, Bones. Get away from them.

My vision is blurry. I blink away the snow. Beside the monument are two men. They're in uniform, guns raised, blocking our way out, and they're marching straight toward us.

I want to kick myself. We should have stayed hidden and moved during the night.

I bend my knees to stand.

"No," says Sam, pulling me back down. "They'll shoot you."

I look around. He's right. There's no cover. Our only option is to get back around the corner and down the ridge. I turn and crawl, burying my elbows into the snow to propel me forward. Sam's by my side.

I sneak a look over my shoulder.

The soldiers are running now, only fifty feet away.

I shimmy forward. My arm plunges into the deep snow. I yank it back out. Adrenaline hurtles through my chest.

Another glance backward. They're almost upon us. I hear the crunch of their boots crushing the snow.

"It's no use," says Sam, his voice raspy.

I want to charge at the soldiers. To knock them down and tell them that we're all on the same side and it doesn't have to be like this. Dad always said that all men are my brothers and all women are my sisters. The photo presses against my skin and I remember what Mom said about the Dalai Lama and nonviolence: *Even in hard situations you must keep your values.*

"Stop!" shouts one of the soldiers. His voice thunders.

I turn. They're almost on us. Four steps away. They move stiffly under the layers of uniform. Fur borders their faces, which wear identical stony expressions. One soldier grips a satellite phone. Snot drips from his nostril. He wipes it away, keeping his gun pointed straight at us.

I stare at him.

He stares back.

I've seen those eyes every day in my memory. They're the same eyes that took Dad.

It's Spaniel.

All thoughts flash out of my head. Blinding anger explodes through me. I lunge forward and glimpse the confusion on his face before I collide with him. I lock my arms around his neck and wrap my legs around his middle.

The other soldier pokes a gun into my side.

"Get away from her!" shouts Sam, scrambling up.

Spaniel coughs, trying to pry my hands off his neck. I smell his stale breath.

"Tash!" shouts Sam.

Hands grab at my back, pulling me. I don't know what my plan was but it's too late to let go.

My fingernails cut into my forearms as I grip them. I kick and my foot makes contact with the soldier behind me.

I catch a glimpse of Sam throwing himself at the soldier attacking him. They fall, tangled on the ground.

My hands are slipping and my shoulders are throbbing. I won't last much longer.

I see Sam scramble away. The soldier raises his rifle. I watch him pull the trigger. He fires.

The gunshot makes a *ting*ing sound.

Sam drops into the snow.

The world stops. I let go. I'm falling, spinning to the ground.

What have I done?

44

ANGER

Hands claw at my clothes, trying to grip my arms.

"Sam!" I scream, wriggling and pushing them away. They grasp my wrists. I can't escape. "Please! I'll do what you want, just let me go to Sam!"

I look up at Spaniel's face. He glares back.

Sam lies motionless, facedown. His head is turned away from me. Blood stains the white snow around his right arm and chest. I search for signs of movement.

Show me you're alive, Sam.

Spaniel yanks my arms above my head.

"Let me go!" I shout, and kick my legs.

There's nothing I can do. They drag me away across the snow, leaving Sam's crumpled body on the ground.

"You shouldn't have killed him," Spaniel says to the shooter. "He's wanted for questioning."

My insides scream that he's not dead. They don't know Sam. He's a fighter.

"Stand!" yells Spaniel. He moves in front of me and lifts me up by my arms.

I let myself go limp and dangle, curling my legs up underneath me. I'm not going anywhere with him.

"Stand," says Spaniel. "Or we'll shoot your friend again."

I don't take my eyes off his as I put my shaking foot in the snow and stand.

The shooter passes him a rope and he fastens it around my waist, clipping both ends to a buckle on his wrist.

We're tied together. There's no escape now.

"Walk," he commands.

I step and my leg folds. My muscles have finally given up. I look back at Sam, lying still on the ground. I have to find a way to get to him.

"We'll take her to the commander," orders Spaniel. "There's no point taking the boy."

"I'm getting out of here," says the shooter. "I've done my bit already."

"Fine," says Spaniel, spitting out his words. "More reward for me."

The shooter marches away. I glare after him. Spaniel walks behind me, pushing me forward.

"Why does it matter to you if I escape? Why can't you just let us go?"

"After I couldn't catch you," says Spaniel, through gritted teeth, "they said I wasn't fit to patrol the town. They sent me out here. You ruined everything." The rifle prods me in the back.

I think back to that night when I hid with Eve. It never occurred to me that the soldiers would get punished if I escaped. I wonder where Wildface and Dagger were sent.

We cut across the snow onto a thin icy path like a knife's edge. I glance down to my right: a vertical drop to rocks below.

"Set me free," I hiss.

"No chance, you little rat," he says, laughing. "The commander will be so happy when I bring you in for questioning."

Anger burns through me. I've had enough.

"We all have to follow the rules," he says.

"But what if the rules are wrong?" I shout at him.

In an instant I understand what Sam meant. It wasn't the Man on Fire's fault that my parents were taken. The police would have found another reason to drag them away.

Steadying my step, I dive suddenly forward. Spaniel stumbles and skids. I'm yanked sideways as he slips off the edge. The rope cuts into my stomach. Throwing my weight in the other direction, I dig my fingernails into the ice to stop myself from toppling over. I lie panting on the ground. I only meant for him to trip, not fall off the path.

Crawling on my stomach, I peer down the side. Spaniel dangles over the edge. He's winded and breathing heavily. He grips the rim with his shaking fingertips. There's terror in his eyes. I know what that looks like now.

I bend forward, unhooking the clip from his wrist. Shimmying backward, I untie the rope from my waist.

I'm free.

INDIA

"**W**ait!" Spaniel calls. "Help me."

He took Mom and Dad and Sam. He's the reason all this happened.

I turn to leave, but I see Mom's face in my mind.

I'm not like Spaniel.

I don't want to kill anyone.

I turn and grab his hand, yanking him up.

"Please," he says.

"I'm trying," I say, grimacing. I'm weak and he's heavy. His fingers are slipping out of mine. My foot finds a hold and I haul him upward. It's just enough for him to get his elbows onto solid ground.

He struggles over the edge of the ridge and collapses in a heap, grasping at the snow.

I yank his gun from him and throw it over the side with all my might. It crashes against the rocks.

Before I know what's happening I'm running as fast as I can toward Sam.

I skid over the ice, not looking back, until the path widens. I squint. There's no sign of Spaniel following me. Taking a deep breath, I carry on. A mist is setting in, chilling the air with it. I spot a patch of scuffed snow.

I see the red bloodstain immediately. It's the only color in the ghostly whiteness.

"Sam!" I shout, dashing toward it.

He's not there. His body has left an imprint in the snow. A red-dotted trail lies beyond it.

He's alive.

I follow the blood spots.

The mist thickens, swamping me in dampness. My heart thuds.

"Can you hear me?" I shout.

"Tash?" he says faintly. "Over here."

I see him, hunched over and grasping his arm. His skin has a gray tinge to it. He shivers.

Bones is standing over him, head lowered. He must have run back to us.

"Where did they get you?" I ask, running over.

He points to his arm.

"Caught the edge," he says between heavy breaths. "My chest feels like it's been punched, though."

His sheepskin jacket is soaked in blood.

I unfasten it and rip back his layers of clothing. His chest is scratched and bruised. There's no bullet wound.

"I thought you were dead," I say softly, taking his good arm out of the jacket before the other. His wound sticks to the material. I slowly peel it back.

Sam sucks in air. The deep cut oozes with clotted blood.

"You'll be fine," I say, ripping my scarf off and tying it around his arm as tightly as possible.

He moans in pain.

I pick up his jacket. An object thuds to the ground. It's the compass. The glass is smashed and there's a dent in the metal. I rub it with my thumb.

"Where was this?" I ask.

"In my front pocket," says Sam. "The bullet must have hit it and ricocheted off."

It saved his life.

"Can you lean on me?" I ask, wrapping my coat around him. "That's the border, over there, see?"

I grasp his clammy hand, glancing over my shoulder to check if Spaniel's behind us. There's no more time to wait.

"Just a few steps and then you can rest."

He props himself against my shoulder and hobbles forward. My body burns under his weight.

"Come on, Bones," I say, glancing behind me. He follows. "Remember the time I broke my ankle climbing the vulture tree?" I have to keep Sam talking, keep his mind off the pain.

He nods. "You had to lean on me and hop on one leg all the way back."

We trudge forward. I wish we could go faster. Every step is agony for Sam but he walks with courage into the unknown.

A red-billed crow pecks at the ground in front of us. It makes a tapping noise with its beak.

"Look, Sam," I say, nudging us forward again. "We have those at home."

"I wish I was home," says Sam.

"We'll get there," I reply.

Even though it's freezing, I'm sweating from trying to keep Sam upright. I don't care if it uses the last of my energy; once we're across, every-thing will be fine. That thought keeps me going.

I check behind me again. There's no sign of movement. No Spaniel creeping up on us.

We reach the monument and are level with the border. The wind rustles the prayer flags as we pass underneath.

"Sam, we made it," I whisper. "We made it to India."

DAWA

I lay Sam down under the shelter of a group of rocks. They jut out of the ground like wolf fangs and remind me we're not out of danger yet.

"Rest now," I say, clearing the loose snow away with my feet. "I'm going to find help." I lean forward to kiss his forehead.

"Hey!" says a voice I recognize.

I jump and stand in front of Sam, blocking him from the man.

"Get away from us," I say, stumbling in the snow. It's the Leader of the nomads.

"I'm not going to hurt you," he says, holding his hands up, surrendering. "Please just trust me."

"What do you want?" I ask. "We're not going back. You can't make us."

The Leader slowly reaches into his bag.

"Don't!" I shout.

"It's just a bandage," he says quickly. "You can come and get it yourself. I only want to check on him."

I nod and he rushes over and examines Sam's wound.

"I didn't realize who you were at first. You were dressed like a boy," he says, dripping water into Sam's mouth before passing the bottle to me. "By the time I did, you'd run away. I've been trying to catch up with you ever since."

"What do you mean?" I ask.

"You were carrying *The Snow Lion*, your father's writing. And you passed us the message from him. I put two and two together."

"It was you who was following us?" I ask.

I knew there was someone out there.

He nods and wraps a temporary sling around Sam's arm. "We need to go."

I look behind me.

Is this a trap?

I can't run any more.

"You know her father?" asks Sam, studying his face.

"We used to be in the resistance together." He turns to me and holds his palm flat beside his knee. "I haven't seen you since you were chubby-cheeked and this high." He smiles at the memory and his mustache crinkles.

"What's he called?" I ask, just to be sure.

"Sonam," he answers without hesitation.

I pause, wrapped in the comfort of hearing Dad's name.

The Leader helped Sam.

I trust my intuition and follow him blindly into the dense mist, leading Bones behind me. My teeth chatter. Sam grips the Leader's shoulder to balance. We descend steeply until we're no longer stepping on snow. I've forgotten what it's like to walk on dry ground and my steps are suddenly light. Bones picks up his pace, happy to be heading downhill.

We walk gradually lower all afternoon, leaving the mist behind and stepping on thin paths through barren mountains sculpted by the wind. Roads curve around the hills in the distance. This side of the border looks similar to home and I long for it.

"My name's Dawa," says the Leader. "It means

'moon.' I move about often and I'm mostly in the mountains with the nomads."

There's a rumble in the distance. A convoy of army trucks appears on the horizon and snakes up the road opposite in a cloud of dust and dirt. They're similar to the Chinese ones but solid green with square fronts.

"We're still in a restricted area, so it's best to remain unseen. We don't have permits," says Dawa, ushering us behind a huge stone jutting out of the side. It looks like a head with dented eye sockets.

Seeing the military makes me uneasy again. My heart thumps. I peer out, watching the trucks get closer. The last passes and through the canvas opening in the back, I spot the silhouettes of soldiers leaning on each other, clasping their rifles.

Once they've disappeared, Dawa leads us onward and we enter a rocky gorge cut by a river.

"I live in the Tibetan community in exile. You should come with me. You'll be safe."

"Does the Dalai Lama live there?" I ask, springing from boulder to boulder, guiding Bones around them.

He nods.

"That's where we want to go!" My voice quavers

with excitement. I instinctively form the secret eagle signal with my hand.

Sam notices and smiles. He waves it back at me with his good arm.

"It's almost over," I whisper.

SAFETY

We reach a village: a cluster of houses nestled between the mountains.

"Is this it?" I ask eagerly.

"We still have a way to go. This is where I left my van."

He turns to Sam. "Just a bit farther; then you can rest."

"Will Bones fit inside?" I ask. My voice sounds stronger, more authoritative than before. "We can't leave him behind."

After standing on top of the mountains, I know that everything is possible.

Dawa steps beside Bones and measures the yak's length with his arm span. Bones shakes his horns at him.

Dawa straightens up. "It will be a squeeze but he should fit."

We stop at a small shop with a slate roof. Four shelves are crammed with juice, biscuits, and food in packets I don't recognize. My stomach grumbles. Beneath them is a gas burner on which a pot of rice cooks.

Outside, goats crowd around a square pool of water, heads down, lapping. I guide Bones to the edge and they part, making space for him.

Sam lies back against the wall, clutching his arm.

A girl with hair in long plaits leans over and speaks to me in Hindi, a language I don't understand. I look to Dawa.

"She's asking if Sam is badly hurt."

I smile at her, feeling shy. "He'll be okay."

She nods and returns to the rice.

Dawa buys biscuits and water. He slides orange-colored notes from his pocket. Each one has a picture of a tiger on it.

The girl strolls over carrying plates of rice and a yellow curry I've never seen before.

I put the food in my mouth and choke. Spice

hits the back of my throat, coating my tongue in chili.

Sam scrunches his face up next to me.

I mix the curry with the rice, trying to make it milder.

"You'll get used to it." Dawa smiles.

My stomach creaks from the food. I wonder if Dawa's right and hope there'll be momos where we're going.

"Make sure you both drink this," says Dawa, dissolving the contents of a sachet into water and handing it to me. "It's for dehydration."

I sip the water. It's salty and citrusy and makes me gag. I pass the bottle to Sam, who eyes it warily.

"It's good for you," urges Dawa.

Bones joins the goats grazing at the side and chews on tufts of grass.

Despite the taste, my body longs for the food and I finish it all. The spice stays in my mouth all through the walk to Dawa's van.

"This is us," he says, standing next to a thin white van.

I blindfold Bones in preparation. He's more docile than before and doesn't protest when I lead him inside, shuffling him right to the front.

There's not enough space for us in the back too.

"Where do we hide?" I ask.

"Hide?" asks Dawa.

I nod.

"We're far enough away from the border, out of the restricted zone. You don't need to hide."

"No one's going to send us back?"

He smiles and shakes his head.

"We really escaped." I let the words sink in.

Sam nods, and even though he's still clutching his arm, his eyes are wide and shining.

I turn to the mountains we just walked from and whisper up to them. "Mom, Dad, I'm coming."

Dawa props Sam next to me and wraps him in blankets. Sam closes his eyes and takes controlled breaths. I wish I could help with the pain.

The van makes a scraping noise before shuddering to life. It rumbles and we bump over rocks. I hold on to the metal handle above me as everyone slides into each other. Sam grimaces. I know exactly how he feels. We'd be safer on our feet.

"Do you know anything about my parents?" I ask. "Or have any news about home?" I tell Dawa about the soldiers taking Mom and Dad.

He sighs. "I'm sorry to hear that. I only knew that the message was coming from him, that's all."

I nod and stare, transfixed, out the front of the van. After a while I get used to Dawa's driving, his steady pace and careful maneuvering around bends.

It's only then that my mind finally lets me close my eyes. For the first time since the soldiers stormed into my home, I feel safe.

MARKET

The van shudders over rocks and I snap open my eyes.

How long have I been asleep?

"Sam?" I ask, turning to him.

My elbow bashes into the metal corner as the van leans.

"We're almost there," he says, gesturing outside. Some of the color has returned to his cheeks. He's holding himself upright and the glazed look on his face has vanished.

I'm angry at myself for drifting off for so long. The truck picks up speed and air flows through the back, making wisps of hair tickle my cheek.

The scenery we're passing is different; the mountains have turned into lush foothills. There are trees everywhere, in all shades of green. It smells of sweet pine. I allow a tingle of excitement to pass through my stomach.

Soon the hills are lined with buildings taller than I've ever seen: houses, shops, and hotels. The empty roads are now crowded with cars, beeping and overtaking each other. A motorbike weaves around our van with a woman in a pink dress and trousers riding it sidesaddle behind a man. Her scarf ribbons behind her.

The salty water must have worked because my head feels clearer.

"How's your arm?" I ask Sam.

He's staring, wide-eyed, at the food sellers lining the road. The oily smell from their pans hits me in a rush of heat.

"Not bad," he says. "As long as I don't think about it."

Relief washes over me. I vow to keep his mind off the pain, thankful there's so much to see.

"What happened to that dog?" I ask, pointing at a pack patrolling the road next to a cow. The dog at the back has no hair and his skin is red and raw in patches.

"Skin disease," says Dawa.

I wish I could help.

A yellow-and-orange truck overtakes us, beeping a melodic tune. Tassels swing in its window. We're side by side, taking up the whole road.

"What if a car comes the other way?" I ask.

"Don't worry, this is normal." Dawa slows to let him pass.

Black smoke streams from the truck's exhaust. I cover my mouth and nose with my coat.

The van climbs uphill again, twisting around hairpin bends. My stomach lurches.

"That's where we're going," says Dawa, pointing at groups of multicolored houses spread over three lush hills. The house walls are light pinks, greens, and oranges. Above the hills are small brown mountains and, behind them, snow-dappled peaks point out. I think this must be the lowest in elevation I've ever been.

We stop on a road enclosed by concrete buildings. A market overflows into the street.

There are people everywhere: behind shop stalls, wandering in and out of the traffic, chatting on benches; monks and nuns in their robes, women in sequined saris, men in suits with round patterned hats.

I close my eyes for a minute, to shelter from it all. It's only when I open them that I realize what's different.

There are no police or soldiers.

No one's afraid.

49

BONES

Dawa opens the door and the air is full of snippets of conversations in languages I've never heard. My ears adjust to new accents.

Dawa helps us out, dodging passing cars. I hear a rustling above me. Snow monkeys bounce on branches. They have black faces framed by a white tufty mane of hair. A baby plays, scampering along a branch and peeping out at me. I could watch them for hours. Dawa nudges me, passing Bones's tether into my hand, and I realize I've been standing in a daze.

"Follow me," he says. "Can you walk?"

Sam nods.

We pass under electric wires tied in big knots that hang overhead. As we wind in and out of the people they stop and look. At first I think they're staring at us, but then I realize they're gaping at Bones. A child runs over and strokes him.

"Do yaks live here?" I ask.

"Usually they live a bit higher up," replies Dawa. "But your yak will be fine here for a while. I'll show you where to walk him up the hill."

Bones's nostrils flare at all the new smells.

We go through narrow alleyways, ducking to avoid overhanging red and blue tin roofs. Prayer flags are draped over everything. Two nuns with shaved heads chatter ahead of us.

I glimpse misty mountains in the distance and instantly feel safer.

"When can we meet the Dalai Lama?" Sam asks.

"He greets everyone who arrives in India from Tibet once a week," says Dawa.

"Once a week?" I ask, stopping in my tracks. "We need to see him now."

"It will be the day after tomorrow," says Dawa.

I think of Mom and Dad and how the soldiers changed our lives in just a few seconds. I have to get there now.

"Where's the temple?" I ask. "I'll go there myself and get him to see . . ."

I stop midsentence. Behind Sam, on the wall, is a blown-up picture of a man surrounded by flames. It's as if I'm back there.

A man on fire.

My body trembles.

Dawa places a hand on my shoulder. "Some people have been offering their bodies to fire," he says. "This man was determined to show the world he wasn't going to suffer under the regime."

"We were there," says Sam.

"We must honor their sacrifice. They act out of love for all people and don't die with anger in their hearts," continues Dawa. "But we must also urge others not to do it."

"Why?" asks Sam.

"It's much better to suffer the things you are suffering in this life and develop compassion, love, and kindness."

That's exactly what Mom and Dad would say. It makes me long for them. I can't blame the soldiers or the Man on Fire. I can't blame anyone. All I can do is try to make things right again.

Sam clenches his fist. "I'll never show the soldiers love," he says. "They took Tash's parents! They shot me and tried to kill me!"

"You can't fault everyone for a few individuals' actions," says Dawa. The evening sun shines on us, showing the lines of strain on his face. "Otherwise you'll face the misery of giving your mind over to anger."

Sam leans his forehead against the picture.

"It's not much farther," says Dawa, beckoning us onward. "We'll get the doctor to come tonight."

I take Sam's good hand in mine and follow Dawa to a small house. The windows have bars across them to keep the monkeys out. A spotted cat meows from the terrace.

"I don't have a stable for the yak," says Dawa. "But there's this courtyard. As long as he doesn't mind sharing with a calf."

The calf watches us with her big brown eyes as we enter.

"Bones needs a new friend," I say, feeling a stab of guilt about Eve.

"Well, that's sorted, then," says Dawa. "He can stay here."

Dawa pays a lady carrying a huge bundle of grass on her back and she bends and places a pile in front of Bones. She has a gold nose ring. I touch my own nose and wonder what it would look like on me. Bones munches on the grass and it pokes out the sides of his mouth.

"Don't worry," I whisper to him, stroking his soft muzzle. "We'll be back soon."

Inside Dawa's house, the first thing I see is a large photograph of the Dalai Lama. He looks older than in my picture. A white scarf is draped over the top of it. Dawa lights a butter candle in front, cupping it with his hand to keep the flame going.

There's a clock on the wall next to it.

"What's the date?" I ask.

"The tenth of November," says Dawa.

Sam catches my eye. I know exactly what he's thinking. The letter said the eleventh. We've got to find out what it means by tomorrow.

CODE

Before dinner, I'm given fresh clothes. In the bathroom, I peel my coat off and Eve's hair scatters onto the floor around me. I frantically gather it up into a bundle and place it back inside the lining, making a note to mend the split seam. I take out the Dalai Lama picture and the ripped copy of *The Snow Lion* from the pocket, keeping them safe.

I stand in the shower, letting the warm water pour over my head and down my back. My feet are bruised and blistered, but I'd have no toes if it weren't for Sam.

Afterward, I stare in the mirror.

I don't even know the girl staring back at me. I touch my face. It feels rough. The parts of it the sun touched are tanned and the skin is burnt and peeling. I think about how far I've traveled and how big the world feels now. I've learned the ways my parents stand up for what is right.

My hair is wild.

You wouldn't recognize me, Mom.

After living outside for so long it feels stranger to be inside than out and that evening we join Bones in the courtyard, not wanting to leave him alone. Dawa carries bundles of wood and builds a fire in the center. He sings softly as he fetches blankets and cushions, and scatters them on the floor before passing us spicy snacks I've never seen before.

Bugs swarm in front of the light in the courtyard.

"We worked out the message in the letter," I say to him.

"I wouldn't have expected anything less."

"But we can't figure out the next bit," says Sam. "Can you help? It says: 'Yaks will fly on the eleventh of November.'"

"That's tomorrow," says Dawa, touching his beard.

I watch intently as he sits and thinks. Sam

and I rest side by side, leaning on Bones. The calf curls up by Bones's feet. My body is tired and achy but my mind is awake and alert.

Eventually Dawa shakes his head. "I'm sorry. My job was just to pass the message on—which, thanks to you, I did. I have no idea what it's about."

"Well, let's start with the date," says Sam matter-of-factly. "Do we know of anything that might be happening tomorrow?"

We all shake our heads.

"Think, Tash. Did you hear your dad say anything?" Sam urges.

"I've thought and thought but there's nothing." I can't help wishing that I'd listened more at home, or asked more questions.

Sam sighs. "Let's check the leaflet again."

We scan the tattered *Snow Lion*.

"The only thing that could be happening tomorrow is the Chinese minister's visit," I say. "But we don't know the exact date—and anyway, why would that be important?"

"Let's keep it in mind just in case," says Sam. "Now what about 'yaks will fly'?"

I shrug. I've thought about it so hard my head spins. Looking out over the town, I watch bright lights twinkle everywhere. It's like nothing I've seen before.

I hug my knees to my chest. There are no lights on the mountains and their darkness looms over us. I look up to the stars and realize I can't see as many as usual.

Dawa hums and I let the tune rock me into a doze. I fall asleep with the leaflet in my hand, dreaming of ministers' visits and flying yaks.

TEMPLE

I wake the next morning and for a second I don't know where I am. The birdsong is different. I hear car horns and drums in the distance. Then I remember Dawa and it all comes flooding back. We made it to India.

I wrap my blanket around me. Today is the eleventh of November and we still haven't figured out the code. The Dalai Lama is my only hope now.

By the time I get up, Sam and Dawa are already sitting eating breakfast. Newspapers are strewn across the table.

"Dawa bought them to see if there was any news."

"Is there?" I ask, joining them, but I can already tell from their expressions that there's nothing.

After breakfast Dawa leads us into town. It seems big. I feel lost and don't know where to start.

"This is the market," he says.

In front of me is more food than I have ever seen. Omelets fry at the side of the road. A woman perches on a step and eats thukpa. Shops sell jars of pickles, chutney, and spices. I peer into one of the restaurants and see plates of colorful Indian food next to glasses of juice.

"What do you think that tastes like?" asks Sam, pointing at a flat round bread filled with potato.

It's all so new it makes me think about how much I don't yet know.

✦ ✦ ✦

The following day, we walk through town to the temple, past street stalls selling prayer beads and brightly colored clothes, and ladies cooking momos on the side of the road.

After the endless silence of the mountains, there's noise everywhere. Cars beep their horns at us to get out of the way. Dogs bark. The air is heavy with smells: incense and spices and burning plastic. I push past the masses in a daze.

At home there was one bus stop. Here there are cars, buses, taxis, and rickshaws.

"That's the kora," says Dawa, pointing to a pathway near the road. "The sacred circuit around the temple."

"I want to walk around it," I say, needing to escape and gather my thoughts.

Sam turns to follow me but Dawa catches his arm. "You still need to rest." He turns to me. "We'll meet you at the temple entrance, okay?"

I nod.

Red monkeys lead the way for me. A mother, followed by a squeaking baby, tightropes across electric wires.

The walk is lined with 108 red prayer wheels, painted in gold, which I spin around clockwise as I pass. I try to do it fast enough that they're all spinning at once. I rehearse my speech under my breath.

"Please help release my mom and dad from prison."

The words sound wrong.

Because it's not just them I want to help.

There are all the other people like them who aren't free either. There's also everyone at home, like Mani and Sam's dad. I think back to Dorjee and his sister who helped me, and to all my neighbors and school friends.

I can't forget anyone.

Can't the Dalai Lama help them all?

The walls are made of flat slates carved and painted with prayers. I know I need all the prayers I can get right now.

Now that I'm finally here, now that we've made it, I'm terrified.

"Hello," says a monk, pressing his palms together.

I give him a little bow and continue. A boy and his small puppy catch up with me.

"What's her name?" I ask.

"Kora," he replies. "I found her here."

She's a ball of fluff that scampers along, biting his feet. I walk behind him, scared to be by myself but unable to face the crowds in town. Next to other people I realize how skinny I've become since we left. I breathe in calmly before hurrying to the steps. I can't be late.

There's a line at the temple entrance. I spot Sam waiting on the top step, tapping his leg. I step forward and stand next to everyone who escaped from Tibet into India.

I had no idea there were so many of us.

The line shuffles forward. Sam pauses in the doorway, hanging back. I grasp his hand and nudge him. Taking a deep breath, I step through the entrance.

We wait in a courtyard under the blue sky. Monks line the balconies above, looking down on us. They remind me of the monastery on the hill by my house, where the gongs sound every morning. I remember the soldiers who surrounded it as I left.

I turn to the person next to us to distract my racing mind. It's a young man with a baby in his arms and a toddler hiding behind his leg.

"Their mother died on the journey," he says, leaning in so the little girl can't hear. "I picked them up and carried them over the mountains with me." Round scars dot his face.

The girl hides behind him, peeking out at me with big eyes.

"Hi, little sister," I say, bending down next to her.

She giggles at me, reaching out a sticky hand and offering a piece of orange.

"Is that for me?"

She nods and her two plaits of hair swing.

I look down at my own hair and force my fingers through the tangled strands.

A silence ripples up the line. I stand on tiptoe and squeeze my head over the shoulder of a person in front.

I glimpse a strip of yellow on deep red robes.
It's him.
The Dalai Lama.

He has a shaved head and big square glasses. He's round-faced and smiling, happy from the inside out.

This is it. We made it.

FLY

I squeeze Sam's hand. His palm is sweaty.

A man with a camera and a huge lens snaps away. People from all over the world walk around the temple on the upper floor. I'd been expecting to be the only one.

"Firstly," says the Dalai Lama, addressing all of us. "I would like to say to each and every one of you, welcome to India."

He moves along the line, getting closer. He smiles the kind of smile I want to be around all the time. I hear him laughing and joking with people farther up. I imagine our conversation and how we will laugh together too.

He reaches Sam, who's holding his hat. The Dalai Lama tries it on, posing for the camera with the earflaps down. He makes everyone feel better.

I bow my head as he approaches. He blesses me with a white scarf. From now on, it will always carry the Dalai Lama's spiritual energy. I think of Mani and pray the blessing reaches him too.

"Welcome," the Dalai Lama says, laying the scarf around my neck. He looks me in the eyes. His hold all the wisdom I expected.

My speech, rehearsed over and over again, vanishes from my head.

"Did you walk over by yourself?" he asks.

I nod.

"Then you must be as strong as a yak." He smiles in admiration.

"Please," I blurt out. "You have to help. My parents are in prison in Tibet."

"I'm sorry, I can't interfere with matters of that kind," he says with a sympathetic smile. "But have hope; it often leads you on unexpected pathways."

This isn't how the conversation was supposed to go.

"Remember your inner strength," he says, turning to the next person.

It's over so quickly. The Dalai Lama reaches

the end of the line and waves goodbye. People clap and cheer.

Sam places his good arm on my shoulder.

I shake him off and run out of the temple, into the crowd outside.

I pause and glance up at the snowy mountains.

Maybe we can go back.

Maybe I can break them out of prison myself.

But I know that it's impossible and suddenly I am lost, with no direction and nothing left to hope for.

I want to be high up away from everyone, back in the mountains.

I break away and head up the hill.

I hear the click of Sam's feet behind me and quicken my pace. I pass an old man holding his hands behind his back, slowly treading up the hill. I rush past tea shops that sell puffed-up bags of chips and mountain crystals. Reaching the pine forest, I'm finally hidden by the big trees.

I press on, leaving the blur of town below me. A stray shepherd dog with a fluffy tail and big paws stops and stares at me, cocking his head to the side.

I stop and climb up into a tree growing out of the side of the mountain, with twisted branches and big leaves. The dog sits by the trunk. I yank the tattered two halves of *The Snow Lion* from my pocket and trace Dad's handwriting with my fingertips. My tears drop onto the paper.

Sam catches up and leans on the trunk, shaking the tree. The leaves float down to the mossy ground. I wipe my nose on my sleeve.

"We'll figure something out," says Sam. "We always do."

Butterflies flutter all about me, mostly red with yellow spots. A different one lands and spreads its wings on a leaf. It's white like a faded crumpled page. All over it are brown lines. It looks like a miniature map. It flutters away into the sky, gone too quickly for me to glimpse it again.

"How will we find our way home?" I ask.

"Remember what the Dalai Lama said," says Sam. "You're as strong as a yak."

I hug the scarf around my neck. I don't feel strong right now. I feel like a failure. The Dalai Lama's words remind me of Dad. He wouldn't expect me to fail. He always says I have the luck of the dragon. *His little yak.*

"Wait," I say, straightening my back. I think of the yaks I have known my whole life. A symbol of strength, an emblem of my country and my culture. "'Yaks will fly.' The yaks are people."

Sam stares at me blankly.

"The people will fly," I say, smiling.

Sam slowly grins. "And flying is like doing the impossible or being set free." He watches a butterfly take off into the sky.

"The prisoners will be set free?"

We beam at each other for a second and then we're racing down the hill, leaping over boulders and swerving around a motorbike coming toward us.

EXILE

Dawa listens to our theory and agrees with us in an instant. He spends the afternoon gathering supplies. When he's ready, he fills the cupboards with rice and noodles for us and passes me the key to the padlock on the front door.

I take his hand. "Find them for me," I say.

"I'll do my best," he says. "I promise."

I look out over the flat roofs down into the valley, watching him disappear into town. I pace up and down the streets and peer into a café crammed with people. Indians, tourists, and Tibetans sit drinking tea. Above the counter is a photo of the Dalai Lama, next to pictures of Hindu gods. Hung against the wall is a Tibetan flag, the same one the Man on Fire held above his head.

I gaze around me. All the objects and teachings that we're not allowed at home are here, displayed in front of me. Shops spill onto the streets selling prayer bowls next to Buddha statues.

The Dalai Lama's teachings aren't passed on in secret but stitched onto wall hangings and sold openly in the shops next to me.

I think of the words I used to blurt out that could have gotten me in trouble, the number of times I whispered *Dalai Lama* into the wind. Here I can say it and nobody cares.

This is what the Man on Fire wanted, this kind of freedom for Tibet.

✦ ✦ ✦

It takes a few days for me to stop the habit of checking over my shoulder for soldiers. Sam and I soon form a routine. First, I look to the mountains and think of my parents and Dawa, willing them to be safe. Then we stroll through the market and wave at the fruit seller, who throws us an apple in return. Afterward, we walk Bones up the hill and leave him to graze until the evening.

The longer we're here the more I realize how hard it will be to go home. The police will still be hunting for us. Sometimes I look at Sam and I know he's worrying about his dad.

"Of course I am," says Sam, when I pluck up the courage to ask him about it. "But I think he'll know where I am and that I'm safe. I reckon Mani or Dorjee's sister told him."

I stare at the ground. "If I knew I'd be saying goodbye for this long I'd have done things differently. I wouldn't have borrowed the yaks," I say quietly, tearing bits of grass between my fingers. "Would you have come with me if you'd known you couldn't go back?"

"Of course," says Sam, meeting my eyes. "But we *will* go back, one day. I'm sure of it."

HOME

The snow falls a month later. It dusts the ground where we are, but completely covers the peaks. I wake after a bad dream and spot the whiteness immediately. My stomach tenses. There's no way they'll make it over the passes. I pull my blanket up to my nose, feeling empty.

"We're running low on supplies," says Sam from the kitchen. "We'll have to change some of that money into rupees soon."

Sam enters and passes me a bowl of porridge. I prop myself up and hold the bowl because it's warm. Nothing will make me hungry right now.

"We should have heard from Dawa," I say.

"Not necessarily. Think how long it took us just to get one way."

"But the snow . . ."

He glances up at the mountains and hesitates.

"Well, I'm not going to feed Bones by myself," he says, giving me a little smile. "If you're not going, I'm not going."

He's got me and he knows it. He stands with his hands in his pockets. I remember my promise to Mani and think of Bones. I swing my legs out of bed and pull on my coats. Once I'm moving I feel a bit better. The cold air blows against my face and the snowy mountains gleam.

This is my favorite time of day to be out, before all the traffic. The shops are just opening and people are outside, cleaning their glass fronts or unpacking boxes of goods on the roadside.

Bones grunts when he sees us and I bury my face in his fur, breathing in his familiar smell. We lead him up the road to graze. His hooves clip-clop on the concrete. Bones knows the route instinctively now and he speeds up when we reach the verge before the grass. He waits at the top, looking toward the mountains, and I know he's pining for Eve. The hawks soar above us.

On days like this we go to the temple and I spin the prayer wheels, remembering the Dalai

Lama. I still keep his picture in my pocket and I reach for it now.

"How many times do you think they've been spun?" asks Sam.

The wheels are worn and faded at the edges, where people touch them.

"Millions."

I think back to when we were on the top of the peaks and how I felt like I could do anything. I take a deep breath and cling to that feeling with all my might, sending it with the prayers to Dad, Mom, Dawa, and the prisoners in the mountains.

On the way back we duck off the main street to avoid the cars and find ourselves in a maze of dark and gloomy back alleys.

I hear a whistle and spin around to look. The whistle brings a thousand memories flooding back, transporting me through time, the way a song does.

Coming down the mountain is a shepherd with a flock of sheep and goats. The animals climb on everything, resting their front legs on rocks to get the highest leaves and sticking out their long tongues.

The shepherd is a short man, wearing a brightly patterned hat. There are three people with him. I see a flash of red.

I shake my head and sigh; all herders must make that noise. I almost thought it was Mani.

I've never seen so many goats all together before. The shepherd whistles again, calling his flock, and I look up to watch the hundred goats and sheep follow him. They don't stick to the path but spread themselves across the mountain, munching as they go.

A woman stumbles and two men rush to help her. I squint.

I stare at the woman, willing her to look up. She's wearing a red skirt. I glimpse her face.

For a second, I can't move. I just stare, in case they disappear.

"Mom!" I shout, leaping toward them. "Dad!"

I'm straining forward with all my weight, running like I used to with Sam, through the barley fields.

It's them. It's really them.

An eagle swoops and dives above me.

I weave around the sheep.

"Mom! Dad!" I run faster and faster, my heart drumming in my rib cage, my body shaking.

My parents look up and see me. Their faces light up.

"Tash?" shouts Dad's deep voice. "Tashi-la?"

I'm nodding and running, arms outstretched.

They hobble toward me, Dawa striding behind them.

I fall into their arms, wrapped in the smell of them and their warmth.

Home. I am home.

I want to hold on forever, to make sure that they are real and never let them go again.

55

HOPE

I usher our little group toward Dawa's house. The buildings gleam in the sunlight. I smile at every person we pass.

Dad's face looks drawn but he still has the same sparkling eyes he's always had.

Sam catches up to us, holding his shoulder. "It's really you," he says, smiling and out of breath.

They link arms with me and Sam and we walk down the mountain together with beaming smiles. A bell jingles and I glance at Mom; my yak bell, the one I thought I'd lost, dangles from a chain around her neck.

"Have you heard anything from my dad?" asks Sam.

They shake their heads. "No," says Mom. "I'm sorry."

"There's been no news since the village was under lockdown," says Dad.

Sam nods. It's just as we'd expected, but it's still hard to hear.

We reach the steps leading to Dawa's. I take Mom's hand and lead her through the door.

I make steaming cups of butter tea and carry them out on a tray, then sit cross-legged on the floor beside my parents.

"What happened?" I ask Dad, bursting to find out. "How did you get out?"

"As you know, my job in the resistance was to write down a code and deliver it to Dawa and the nomads." He leans back in his chair. "I failed the night the Wujing came, but you delivered it to the nomads anyway."

"'Yaks will fly on the eleventh of November,'" I say.

"Exactly," says Dad. "It was the date of the visit from the Chinese minister, the only time the police would be distracted. It was the day the prisoners were to be set free."

"So it all went according to plan?" asks Sam.

"Yes, and it was all thanks to you, don't you see? You set us free." Dad is beaming.

"Not only that," says Mom, "but we got lost in the mountains. If Dawa hadn't found us we never would have made it."

I smile at Sam and squeeze his hand. We knew the code was important.

"Where are the other prisoners?" I ask.

"They stopped to rest in a village we passed earlier," says Dawa. "Your parents insisted on coming straight here."

"We had to see you both," says Mom.

I sip my butter tea, letting the news sink in.

"Your dad is the only person in the resistance who knew when the minister was coming," continues Mom, leaning forward and taking my hand. "The government kept it secret so that no one could plan any disturbances or protests."

Dawa stands and lights four incense sticks. The smoke curls upward, filling the room with the scent of a temple.

"The resistance has been planning a prison break for some time," says Dad, smiling. "You made it happen."

It seems so obvious now that I wonder how we didn't figure it out sooner.

Suddenly the pain of the journey is gone. Dad

grabs my hand and spins me around. I laugh.
Mom and Dad look at each other fondly.

I did it.

I set them free.

I look around for Sam. He's outside with
Dawa, leaning over the balcony and quietly
staring at the mountains. They glisten under
the bright blue sky. He turns and spots me. His
hand forms the secret eagle sign. I smile and
signal it back at him.

I think of the Dalai Lama and remember his
words.

Hope leads us on unexpected pathways.

A hawk soars, surrounded by ravens.

Mom's hair has come loose and it waves behind
her in the breeze drifting through the door. She
lifts the yak bell from her neck and smiles with
her deep brown eyes.

"I carried this for you," she says, placing the
yak bell over my head, lifting my hair out of the
way. It's cold against my skin and I tuck it under
my sweater.

I'll give it to Mani when we finally get home.

Facts About Tibet

- Tibet is the source of five of Asia's largest rivers, providing water for over one billion people.

- "Hello" in Tibetan is *tashi delek*.

- In Tibet only a male yak is called a yak; the female yak is called a *dri*.

- In Tibet a spiritual teacher is called a Lama. A Dalai Lama is the head Lama within Tibetan Buddhism. There have been fourteen Dalai Lamas so far.

- China's invasion of Tibet began in 1950.

- Over one hundred thousand Tibetans have fled their country, risking their lives to become refugees in India, Nepal, and elsewhere.

- The act of offering oneself as a sacrifice by fire is called *self-immolation*. Since 2009, there have been more than 140 self-immolation protests in Tibet.

Acknowledgments

To everyone at Algonquin Young Readers, thank you for turning this story into a beautiful book, especially Elise Howard, for believing in it in the first place. The book has found its perfect US home.

To my UK editor at Orion, Fliss Johnston, for shaping the story, along with Julia Sanderson and Lena McCauley—thank you. My wonderful agent, Sallyanne Sweeney, thanks for your support, expertise, and advice. Thank you to Jason Cohen, for my author photo; Carla Weise, for a cover design I adore; and Jim Madsen, for such gorgeous artwork.

Thanks to everyone at the Library of Tibetan Works and Archives, and to Robert Thurman, for allowing me to draw from your statement on self-immolation in Dawa's dialogue.

Thanks to my Bath Spa MA writing for young people peers and continuing workshop groups, and to my incredible writing tutors, Steve Voake, Julia Green, Lucy Christopher, Janine Amos, and John McLay.

Thanks to my friends and family on both sides of the pond: to my parents, Anya and Mark; to my sisters, Rachel, Olivia, and Hazel, for sharing adventures; to Anne, Rick, Dan, Emily, and Jon J.; to my grandmas, Mary Burke Roche and Jean Butterworth, for being my light; and to my husband, Jonathan, for always bringing support and inspiration.